I0733407

FATED WOLF

SAVAGE SERIES

MILA YOUNG

CONTENTS

JOIN MY VIP NEWSLETTER!

A FREE STORY JUST FOR YOU ....

SAVAGE SERIES

Lost Wolf

Broken Wolf

Fated Wolf

Cursed Wolf

FATED WOLF

Everything I've been taught my whole life has been a lie...

Hate is a cruel word...but finding out what my mother has done... what's she's hidden from me is unforgivable.

Add to that, the four men I've let into my life have been keeping secrets from me too.

I have a few truths of my own to reveal that might change everything between us.

With the threat of war darkening our world and my ex fated mate on our heels, I don't see how we can survive if we let the past break us apart.

Can I find a way to forgive them before it's too late and I lose everything?

Fated Wolf is set in the same world as Shadowlands Sector, with some cross over of characters. This series can be read without having read Shadowlands first.

NARAH

"I don't give a fuck if you're in pain or crying," Martell barks, his stale breath brushing over my face. "You are not getting away from me this time."

Lowering my chin into my chest in desperation, I refuse to let my fated mate see my tears. He lost the privilege when he threw me off a cliff. He shattered my existence the moment he rejected me, separated me from my sisters, and I've been on the run ever since.

Now, look at me. I'm back with this monster, who the universe decided deserved to have my wolf crave and to share my heart with. I never understood how the wolf goddess could have paired me with such a loathsome man, how we have nothing in common, yet our wolves call to one another. Even now, mine whimpers within my body, knowing who stands in front of us.

I hate Martell, but I hate my body more for wanting this asshole. My chest sticks out to him for his touch, making me both sick and aroused.

My toes barely scrape the cement floor of the basement with my wrists tied to chains over my head. This mother-fucker has me imprisoned, and I'm trembling with anger.

For the dozenth time, I reach deep inside for my magic, for the power Mother said made me a sorceress, but it's as though all my magic has been scooped out of me. I'm empty, and an empty ache flares in my gut that it's all her fault. She took my power before Martell's wolves killed her, so how can I ever find out the truth?

He grabs my chin and squeezes, his fingernails digging into my flesh until I groan. Pushing my head back, he studies me with a leering look in his eyes. His short, dark hair is parted on the side, and he's grown a dark beard since I last saw him.

His hostility toward me hasn't changed, though.

"You don't deserve me as your fated mate," he growls, then sniffs me, his nostrils flaring. "Especially a cursed like you who's let other Alphas rut her. I knew you were a fucking whore."

"Fuck off!" I never asked to be born half-wolf, half-witch and never wanted him as my fated mate. Thing is, being cursed makes me the lowest of scums in the eyes of most wolves. I'm not a pureblood wolf shifter or full witch, so I'm an outcast in both worlds.

Martell sneers, his lips curling away from his yellowing teeth. A mountain of strength towering over me, his eyes are dark as the pits of hell. He's not the most handsome man, not with his thin, dried lips, oversized head, and his twisted features when he scowls. Apparently, when it comes to fated mates, what matters to our wolves are carnal connections.

"You think you can hurt me?" I say, finding my courage. "Let me go, or you'll regret ever touching me," I snarl. Maybe it's foolish, but I'm no longer the meek girl he once knew. The ache of finding my mother again and being betrayed by her, then losing her, has changed me.

In the past, I pretended to be someone different, someone who was meek and obedient to the Storm Wolves, but that person is long gone.

Fragments of the past flood my thoughts, raising my anger further—my mother dying at the hands of Martell's wolves, me being kidnapped while my sisters remain in potential danger. Ragnar comes to mind, as do the other three men who I've grown too attached to lately. I don't even know if they are alive, but I grind my teeth, needing to believe they aren't dead. I blink the tears away, knowing that letting myself drown in pity and panic will get me killed quicker.

Martell seizes me by the throat, pulling my face closer to him while my whole body shudders.

"You think you're in any position to threaten me?"

His grip tightens, and my breaths lock in my lungs. I writhe against him as my chest burns up from the despair to breathe again. With adrenaline, I kick out my bound feet, striking him, but he doesn't react. He holds my gaze like the monster he is while darkness feathers the edges of my vision. The way he studies me is reminiscent of the rogue wolves who see women as only to be used for rutting. I live in a deadly world where we are possessions to be sold and used.

Magic... that's the only thing that could give me a slight advantage against Martell. The one thing I don't have.

"It's time to right some wrongs," he murmurs.

I jerk my head up to look at him, dreading to find out what he's talking about.

"Initially, I intended to kill you, but I might have been a bit rash. I have a better use for you, my little slut. My men are starved of females, and seeing you spread your legs to any cock, well then, I'll toss you to my men."

My stomach tenses, my head spins from the lack of oxygen, and his words are a dagger shredding my heart. I'll take my own life before I let him or any of his men touch me.

"How does that sound?" He arches a bushy eyebrow.

I thrash in response, needing air. It's all I care about.

He abruptly releases my neck with a growl.

Gasping for air, I greedily suck in air into my empty lungs while he snatches my hair and forces my head to nod.

"G-Go fuck yourself," I wheeze.

"This filthy mouth of yours is new, Narah. Something I'll have to fix."

This asshole is a real piece of work. His words fill me with dark thoughts while air saws in and out of my lungs. I try to blink as my heart thunders as if someone's punching me in the chest. On our first night together, I craved his attention, to have him want to know everything about me and promise me the world.

I'd been foolish, not knowing any better.

The way he looks at me now belongs to a man who's unhinged, unstable. Still, my wolf cries for him, and I know his wolf does as well. I see it in his eyes, but he doesn't seem to care.

The bite mark Ragnar gave me to suppress my wolf's pining does nothing to keep my wolf's hunger at bay any longer.

I imagine dragging my fingernails across Martell's face and the pleasure I'd take. Once again, my wolf snarls against me. She's confused and lost to the mate bonding, but if she knew better, she'd want to rip his throat out, too.

"I will never give you anything." My words are barely a raspy hiss as I still struggle for breath.

He lifts a blade in his hand, and my muscles tighten. In my blurry vision, all I can focus on are his perfect teeth as his lips twist in warning. The tip of his blade skims across my collarbone, scraping skin, tearing it. Flinching, I bite my tongue to stop from screaming. He fists my shirt and rips it open, then makes quick work of cutting it off me as he strips me. I wrench back because his blade nicks flesh as he slices material until I'm left only in my underwear and bra.

"Nothing you do will change that you're a fucking pig," I cry, my whole body trembling, teeth chattering, while loose tears fall down my cheeks. I hate to show him any weakness, but the emotions pouring out of me are fueled by rage, by how much I want to hear Martell wail in pain.

He lets out a dark laugh. "Don't kid yourself to think you have any sway over me. My wolf might long for you, but my disgust for you revolts against the bond." He raises his knife in a flash, then slashes across the top of my chest.

I scream while the sting burns. The thought has my heart thumping, my wolf growling against me.

"I want to speak to Lovis," I manage between the sobs with as much steel in my voice as I can muster.

"That old fuckwit is dead," Martell scoffs. "I took his place as head Alpha of Storm Wolves. He won't save you... no one will."

His response rattles me. Not that Lovis was a good man, but growing up, he had shown me sympathy and would have been a better man to negotiate with.

"I will never be yours."

"I never wanted you," he snaps.

My wolf whines at his words.

Narrowing my gaze on him, he backhands my face. Stars blind me, and I lurch backward from the strike. The sharp pain reverberating through my skull never ends but pulses across my face. I cry out louder and feel the shackles around my wrist loosen.

He's removing the chains around my wrists.

The sting across my face and my chest have me collapsing to the ground when my legs give out. It's a strange sensation to feel as if I might have a concussion after that one hit but still have my wolf whine for this asshole. Shaking my head to clear my vision only makes the room spin faster.

"I have a surprise for you," Martell states with a promise to make me suffer. He crouches and slices his knife through the ropes binding my ankles together. "Not that I should bother telling someone as pathetic as you, but this will bring me more enjoyment than you."

On his feet, he snatches my hair, fisting it. Agonizing pain sparks across my skull, and I grab his hand to ease the pain while clumsily scrambling to my feet. My stomach squeezes as I stumble after him. Injuries will heal, but I can't control my wolf's mating bond while we're close, how my wolf moans for him, or the heartache curling around my heart.

Father once told me fated mates were a gift from the moon goddess. To find our perfect match in a world flooded with despair is the beacon of light everyone seeks. How can I believe that when mine is ready to literally throw me to the wolves?

Martell drags me through a dark hallway, and I punch his arm, screaming for release, but my voice only echoes around us. In his hurried rush, I trip on the stairs we're climbing, my knees strike the sharp edges, and the pain ripples up my legs. The bastard never ceases despite my cries.

Moments ago, we were in the dark basement, but now bright light stings my eyes. Standing on the front porch of his home, close to fifty pack members, all male, crowded in the dusty yard. They're frozen in place, their attention pinned on me.

The sight strangles me, and breathing is close to impossible.

Martell shoves a palm to my back, and I lurch forward but catch myself from going down the steps. The hunger in their eyes devours every inch of my body. Martell fists my hair and moves to stand alongside me, looking at his men.

"As I promised you, I have brought back the slut who abandoned us," he roars.

Except he's lying, isn't he? He must not have told his pack he threw me off a cliff to die because he knows they'd turn against him if he did. Females are scarce in our world, so most males will never find a mate or someone to rut. As much as we're hated, we are a necessity. If they discover he attempted to kill me, they'll turn on him.

Just as the last Alpha of Storm Wolves killed my father, blaming him for my mother running from the pack.

I glare at Martell. While screaming the truth would bring me joy, I'm also not a fool to think his men would believe me over him.

"Narah has committed a crime, and for that, I reject her as my fated mate," he crows. "So, she will soon be yours to share. Too many of you are denied a female, and this is my gift to you. No man should ever be without a female to rut."

The men hoot and bellow like wild animals. I want to scream and run from the pack I once called home. The place I grew up with my sisters, where my parents kept us safe.

Martell tightens his grip, and I yank against him.

"I'll die first," I hiss.

"You are too precious to die." He grins with his teeth showing.

Trembling, rage pulsing through me, bile scratches the back of my throat at his sugary words.

A wind blows past me, like invisible hands tearing at my hair just as hard as Martell pulls, and the world shifts around me. Staring at the ravenous males has my skin crawling, and a sense of defeat flares over me.

One push from Martell, and I'll be attacked.

"Give her to us," a tall man calls out, then licks his chapped lips. "We'll take her off your hands."

I instinctively step backward.

Martell snarls, and I shudder as desperation overwhelms me. Perspiration runs down my back, and a frantic sensation floods my veins. Looking at Martell, I implore him to have mercy.

"Don't do it. I can be of help to you." My self-loathing at begging this monster leaves me sick to my stomach, but sometimes, desperation makes you weak. Even a snake recoils when in danger, waiting for just the right moment to strike.

The men grow rowdier, and I can't stop trembling.

I loathe Matrell... despise him. He's the epitome of hatred, yet in his presence, unmerciful energy floods me, reminding me we're fated mates.

Raising his chin to his men, he responds, "Prepare for a celebration tonight. She will be yours officially after a ceremony."

I shake all over and wrench against his hold. My heart thunders, and my palms are slick with sweat as panic carves through me. The sick asshole promised me to his pack, and they're salivating. I yank my head back, needing to get out of here, to find a weapon, anything...

Seconds pass, but they feel like hours before Martell swings me around by my hair and drags me back into the house. I barely sense walking or the pain he's causing me. I'm too close to crying uncontrollably, unsure how much more I can tolerate.

Ragnar. I bellow for him in my mind to come for me, to bring carnage to Martell and his pack.

The basement smells of damp and mildew when he swings open the door. He shoves me inside with a hand at my back, and I stumble forward, tripping on my own feet before I fall to my knees.

"You're right," he snarls behind me with a venomous voice. "I need something from you, and if you don't want my men to rip you apart tonight, you'll do everything she says."

Wait! She?

My stomach sinks as panic rises. Twisting my head around to face the doorway, a young woman, dressed in dark riding pants and a buttoned-up jacket, walks into the basement. There's no missing the black mark at the center of her brow, marking her as a witch, just like others I'd seen. I have no idea who she is or why she's here, only that her presence means danger.

"Hello, Narah," she sing-songs and shuts the door behind her, closing Martell out.

"What do you want?" I hiss through clenched teeth.

2

RAGNAR

The dark forest is bare of enemies. The ones I have found are dead, and I'm shuddering with rage that they ambushed us. I'm an idiot for letting my guard down... so fucking stupid.

Night surrounds me, lofty trees bleeding into the blackness, and everything remains deathly still as though I've found myself in a vacuum of darkness. Shit escalated fast and caught us off-guard. The wolves emerged from the shadows, their numbers tripled ours, but we turned into monsters, slaughtering every one of them, yet it wasn't enough. They were just a decoy for what they really wanted.

My Narah.

Fear flares in my chest, and darkness slithers under my skin.

Catching a hint of her scent—the most fucking delicious scent I've ever smelled—I abruptly veer to my right. It vanishes fast. Hell! I sniff out other wolves who'd been here, all male, but the smell barely lingers on the light wind, swallowed by the pungent sting of blood left by the dead.

From the first time Narah approached me in a bar with her proposal to find her sisters, I lost myself to her. I realized later I'd fallen for her, and now I'm left with broken fragments of memories of her, of our time together, etched into my soul.

When I fucked her in the woods, marking her, making her wolf forget her fated mate, I should have known one time with her would never be enough. That no matter what I told myself, I wouldn't be content until I took her as mine. I crave to kiss her full lips, lick the curve of her neck, caress her breasts, and stroke the fire between her thighs.

Breathing hard, I do a loop around the house, following the scents, only to come back to the dead body on the worn track—Narah's mother never stood a chance against the wolves. Her throat was torn out, her life stolen. The gaping wound on her neck still bleeds, with dark rivulets of blood running down the sides of her neck and sinking into the soil. She smells of death already. How long before she turns into an undead?

They wanted her out of the way to get Narah, wanted the danger of her magic eradicated.

The longer I stare at her lifeless body, the more memories flood my thoughts of the fierce battles I'd faced—blood splattered across my face as I ripped the enemy to pieces, their screams and pleas deafening me. My body stiffens in an odd way. Those fights had never bothered me before today. I'd slay and move on. Death has always been part of my life, a moment in time when a soul blinks out of existence.

Death is life.

Words my father lived by, and his father and so on. From a young age, he taught me when you go into battle, you do so as if you're already dead, so you have nothing to fear. In the afterlife, you join those who left too early, and you go into battle with valiant ferocity.

Yet the longer I stare at the woman at my feet, the more I see Narah on the ground, twisted and broken. Is this her, somewhere else?

Something squeezes my heart.

Coldness runs down the length of my spine, and I shiver.

We hadn't been prepared.

We let ourselves be distracted.

We should have known better.

Fuck!

Footsteps close in behind me, and I lift my gaze to see Stone crossing the dark woodland, coming my way. Behind him, the ground is littered with slain wolves. Nikos and Crius are going over the bodies to see if any of the enemies still live. We lost control. I lost myself to rage when we should have kept one man alive to find where they took her.

"Anything on Narah?" I demand, hopeful he found something.

He shakes his head, his stark expression pale, while blood stains his brow, and more blood drips from the long scratch on his neck, which tells me everything. A deep, unsettling ache presses beneath my breastbone.

"She's gone," he growls. "Those motherfuckers stole her from us." His shoulders bunch up, and he's ready to lose his shit again... we all are. No one takes anything from us.

Fear for her life flares through me, smothering me. Having her taken buries me in emotions I never expected I'd feel for her. The hollow in my chest expands from how much I miss her smell, the sound of her laughter, the softness of her body against mine. Even breathing hurts. Over the course of the past few weeks, she's become entrenched in our lives. I exhale loudly with the frustration suffocating me.

Stone clenches his jawline, agitated.

"We'll find her," I say. "I'll burn down this whole cursed world to find her." My hands shift into my wolf, white fur rushing up my arms and long claws extending with desperation. I hold back the rest of the transformation, knowing I need my head screwed on without losing my shit to my wolf. The painful desperation to charge into the woods to search for her like a maniac pummels into me, but what will that achieve?

"Do another round of the woods. Anyone stands in your way, cut them down," I holler. Shaking my arms, my wolf retracts.

"Scents are everywhere," he states what I already know. "The blood all over the woods is throwing us off their scent."

"That's not good enough," I growl. "Find them."

Without another word, Stone turns and pushes back into the woods, barking the order to the other two men.

Scouring the land, I march along the worn track past the house, I assume belongs to Narah's mother. So, where the fuck is my little fox? The air is absent of her sweet scent. Only the acrid smell of magic from Narah's mother, blood, and other wolves fills my nostrils. I know Narah's not here, but I search for a clue which direction they went.

I push into a run once more, taking a wider sweep around the sloped landscape. Wolf Mountains Village sits on the side of a mountain, and I come to a halt when I catch a sight of the open landscape at the base of the mountain.

No movement beneath the moon's gaze below. No sign of the assholes escaping with Narah. Not a fucking thing in sight.

Something unwanted unfurls inside me—panic that she's lost to us.

Tilting my head back, I unleash a harrowing howl with the promise of death to those who dared cross me and take what's mine.

My last conversation with her had been an argument about her fucking my men and that she was mine. Now, the fight strangles me. Hindsight is such a bitch. I'd give her anything she desired to have her back, to keep her safe by my side.

Following the path down to the Wolf Mountains' entrance and returning empty-handed, I quicken my pace. Something in my gut tells me we aren't dealing with random wolves attacking us to steal a female for rutting. The ambush had been orchestrated, and everything points to the Storm Wolves.

Apparently, Narah's fated mate didn't get the message that she was ours. We slaughtered his men, and the bastard returned.

I launch myself madly into the woods, running with the manic beat of my heart, snarling with each heavy inhale. I don't know how long we search the woods, slashing through the forest, trying to pick up anything that might give us a direction they went, but it's all in vain. Gritting my teeth, I come up short, and my chest fills with the rise of panic. We have no leads, no direction to follow.

"Where the fuck can she be?" Nikos roars. His arms are stiff by his side, and he's shaking with the fury glaring in his eyes.

"Storm Wolves took her." Crius cracks his neck, joining us, along with Stone. "I'm certain of it."

"Then we go hunting," Stone's voice darkened, his expression twisted with rage. He knows as well as I do that Narah's in deep shit, and the longer she's missing, the higher the chance that bastard could kill her. Heat pours off Stone.

"And which direction would that be?" Nikos snaps. "We'll go in circles."

Frustration bursts over me. "We can't keep running in circles like this. We may need to split up. First, let's quickly move the witch's body into the house before she turns into an undead and goes ballistic on the locals. We'll tie her up." I may be a bastard, but I won't unleash an undead on the local village.

"She deserves to be burned. She killed us to remove that curse and distracted us," Crius grumbles under his breath.

"Calm down." I lower my voice. "Let's just get this done, then we can get going."

It takes no time to pick up the witch and carry her into the house. I can only assume this is her home, considering the river where she uncursed us backs up to the house.

"She still hasn't changed. That's strange, right?" Nikos states, his voice heavy with a thread of intrigue more than fear.

Stone and Crius have her in their arms, shuffling along the path toward her house.

"Maybe you should carry her then?" Stone gripes.

"You're doing fine," Nikos rebuts. "I just find it weird she hasn't gone all zombified yet."

"I bet she put enough spells on herself to avoid coming back as one," Crius grumbles. "What happens if a powerful witch returns from the dead, anyway? I mean, have you seen any witch zombies?"

"How can you tell if they were once witches?" Stone quizzes.

"Just hurry up," I grit out.

"Yeah," Stone adds. "I don't need her snapping awake and biting my balls off."

Crius snorts, seeing he's holding her feet.

I push ahead of them and open the front door of the wooden cottage. It's a quaint, one-story place made of dark logs. White curtains cover the windows, and it has a small chimney. There are other homes in these woods, but this one is mostly isolated. Entering a small mudroom, boots are lined up on a small wooden shelf, and coats hang off hooks on the wall.

Stone opens the door into the home, sticks his head inside, and makes a hissing sound. He looks back at us over his shoulder, his nose scrunched up.

"Something reeks. It's bad."

Pushing past the guys, the heavy decay of death hits me.

What in the world has the witch been up to? Allie, Narah's mother, appeared like any normal wolf shifter when I first met her in the town, guarded but not threatening. Now, I suspect there is a lot about Narah's mother we don't know.

Beyond the doorway is a large room with a gas oven and wood counter against the wall on the right, then a cozy hearth, where flames flicker and crackle. The fireplace lights up the room, throwing shadows across the wood walls, and something catches my attention. Someone is sitting on the sofa, their back to us.

I stiffen, then glance over my shoulder at my men and whisper, "We're not alone. Set her down and stay guard. Nikos with me." Nikos and I enter the room.

"Hello," I say loudly, irritated. I don't want to deal with this right now, but I need to ensure this is Allie's house before I leave her dead body in here. When there's no response or movement, I exchange a look with my second in command. He shrugs and raises his voice with confidence.

"Who are you? We have some bad news about the witch we believe lived here." Stone gags from the stench but holds it together.

Silence. My skin ripples—something feels off.

Not having the patience for this, I flick my hand to Nikos to round the couch on his left, and I'll take the right. We move hastily and loop around to face the sofa, and I stop at the sight in front of us. An undead man—sunken cheeks, darkness beneath his large eyes, lips so thin they might as well not exist, body so scrawny, his clothes hang off bones—lounges in the seat as if the creature is playing homemaker. White hair is combed off his face as if someone took the effort to brush it for him.

He's staring into the fire, paying no attention to us.

My skin shivers at the sight.

"What the fuck is this?" Nikos grumbles.

"It's not chained up."

"Maybe it stumbled in here," Nikos adds.

"And what? Decided to keep warm by the fire. Why isn't it attacking us?"

"I'll fix that." Nikos draws a blade from his belt, takes several steps forward, and lashes a hand to its throat, pinning him in place to avoid being bitten. The creature doesn't fight him, not even a flinch. These creatures are anything but docile. They attack anything moving, ravenous monsters who kill everything and infect those they bite.

Except this one.

Oddly enough, the man lifts his gaze to Nikos, and call me crazy, but there's life behind them.

Sympathy.

His mouth opens, making a gurgling sound.

Nikos raises his blade. "That's enough of you."

"A-Allie," he gurgles.

"Stop." I lunge and grab Niko's arm as it swings it for the man's face. "Something's not right here."

"You don't fucking say," he growls.

"No, he just said the witch's name. Have you ever heard an undead talk?"

Nikos blinks at me, then glares at the man he's holding by the throat.

"A-llieeee," the man groans, sounding almost mournful.

An idea strikes me, one as simple as observing what will happen if he sees her.

"Bring the witch in here," I order. "Place her in front of him."

Nikos still holds the man by the neck, locked to the sofa, and leans forward. "What is wrong with you?"

"A-Allieeee."

"It's broken," Nikos says. "I mean, what has the witch been doing? Spelling it to not go into a frenzy on her ass?"

"Maybe she's working out a way to combat them," Crius adds as he shuffles inside, carrying the witch with Stone.

He has a point. What other explanation is there?

Placing the witch on the gray rug in front of the couch, the firelight dances over her limp body, illuminating the blood on her cheek and neck. Her skin has already paled. Anyone else would have reanimated.

What have you been playing with, witch?

"A-llieeee," the man screeches, arms reaching for her.

"What the hell's it doing?" Stone asks.

"Grieving?" Crius suggests.

"Let him go," I say.

"You sure?" Nikos asks, his voice firm.

"It's four against one. We can take on one undead if he turns on us."

In a flash, Nikos retracts his hand from the zombie's neck and jumps away from the couch.

Crius chuckles under his breath.

The man throws himself off the couch with unexpected speed, which has me reaching for my blade. One bite and you'll change into these pathetic creatures.

On his knees, he leans over the witch's body, bony ridges from his spine pushing against his shirt like an arched bridge, and paws at her stomach.

I exchange worried looks with Nikos. "Is he going to eat her?"

His eyebrow arches.

"Those are odds I'd bet on," Crius blurts.

The man's pulling at her clothes as if he's digging for treasure, his mouth making slurping sounds that sicken me.

"Okay, this is enough," I demand.

"Shit, I don't need to see him feeding on a corpse. Get it off her," Stone shouts.

Nikos and I hurry forward and grab the undead by his shoulders, wrenching him backward, but his strength is extraordinary, and he resists. Partially dragging him off the woman, I see he's grasping to get hold of a vial half sticking out of her pocket. There's no blood, no eating or tearing of flesh.

"Stone," I bark. "Get your ass over here." In seconds, he's at my side. "Grab the vial from her pocket."

He moves at lightning speed, and the man lurches after Stone, bony hand reaching for him. Stone recoils, his back hitting the wall.

"Give it to him," I instruct, and he practically throws it at him.

The zombie snatches the small glass container from a shaky hand. The cylinder-shaped container is filled with what looks like blood, and the man makes a lip-smacking sound that gives me goosebumps. Not much scares me, but these things have me gagging.

We hover around him, watching as he sits back on his knees, tears the cork off, and presses the vial to his lips. He slurps the contents as they rush into his mouth. Eyes closed, he wrenches backward, tapping the base of the vial with his other hand as his tongue laps into the glass container, licking the edges.

Stone makes a retching sound, and the hair on my arms lifts.

An acidic scent of magic slithers around me, coming from the man—something dark, something inhumane, something powerful.

The vial slips from his grip and tumbles across the rug, bouncing several feet toward Stone's boots before pausing. When the zombie arches his chest forward, bones crack, and his whole body contorts.

Nikos gasps, stepping backward. "Do we kill it now?" he snarls.

"Not yet." I need to understand what's going on. We know so little about zombies, aside from how to kill them. What if Allie learned something about these abominations in our world? Maybe how to stop them or overpower them. Better yet, how to control them.

"Pull back," I say to my men as the man thrashes and growls. His face appears unnatural, and when his head jerks up, I notice he's changing. Sunken cheeks puff out, pasty blue skin lightens to a pink color, lips pillow out, and his body grows, filling his clothing.

"What the fuck am I looking at?" Crius murmurs, trepidation shaking his voice. Nothing scares Crius except his own life, so this is new.

"He's coming back to life," Nikos states matter-of-factly, though we don't really know what's going on.

In moments, the man's posture straightens, his chin lifts, and his eyes blink. I might almost believe he might be alive. Almost. He turns to each of us with golden-hazel eyes, his brow furrowing, and appears slightly perplexed. His attention lowers to Allie, then back to me. There's no grief or agony on his face. He's a statue, void of emotion. There's nothing behind his gaze, just a soulless vessel.

"Are you here to help my wife? She needs to keep feeding me," he says flatly, his tongue slipping out and licking a drop of blood from his lip. His voice is barren of any sentiment.

"Wait the fuck up!" Nikos blurts. "This man, this zombie, is Allie's husband? Does that mean..." He stares at me, bewildered. "He's Narah's father?"

"No way," Stone murmurs. "Didn't Narah say her dad was killed, and she buried him on the land of her old pack?"

"That's what I thought." Yet I'm bristling at the sight of the undead man, appearing and speaking like a normal man. He's staring at us, waiting for an answer.

A response we don't have.

My men are silent, which never happens, a testament to how fucked up the situation is.

3

NARAH

Fear is toxic.

It makes you its slave... something I've lived with my entire life, and I hate it.

So, as much as I can help it, I won't show this witch I'm afraid. Growing up, my father taught me card games that included bluffing, and I've mastered the skill since leaving the Storm Wolves. Raising my gaze to the witch in Martell's basement, I show her nothing.

"What do you want?" I demand in a clipped voice.

The woman with deep brown hair tucked behind her ears stares at me, her pale gaze intense. Her features are delicate, small chin and nose, even her ears are tiny. There's almost an innocence about her, which can't be right. Unless she's another of the High Priestess' hostages.

I wouldn't put it past Lyra to have cursed the whole coven under her command, just as she has my sister.

"It may not seem like it, but I can be of help to you, Narah," she whispers. Her gaze moves frantically around the basement, then settles on the door before she returns my way.

"I wasn't born yesterday." I snort, crossing my arms across my chest, standing in my bra and underwear. "What do you really want?"

In a flurry, she rushes past me. I flinch and regret my obvious jumpiness, but this woman, who looks to be in her early twenties or younger, doesn't notice. Why would Lyra send her? Her power must be extraordinary.

Several feet away from me, she picks up the scraps of blue fabric from the floor that was once my dress, which was torn off by Martell. I wince at the thought of how he treated me, of his promise to toss me to his men. Clenching my jaw, I want him begging for mercy for all the things he's done to me. Then I'll shove him off a cliff edge.

The faint sound of the witch's murmurs distracts me. I lick my lips, then the bite of magic races down my arms. Letting out a ragged gasp, I retreat from her, sliding toward the door. I won't end up like Kaira—a puppet to the High Priestess—not in my lifetime.

When the witch pivots to face me, I tense all over, expecting a torrent of magic to stream in my direction. Instead, she's holding my dress, no longer in shreds but whole as if it was brand new. Confused, I blink at my clothing, then at her.

"I'm Piper," she says, her jaw ticking as she makes her way toward me and pushes the dress into my hands. "Quickly, we don't have much time." Her hand extends toward the door, and a spark of electricity zips to the entryway and spreads across the frame.

"What did you just do?" I gasp as I slip into the dress. I don't know what this witch is up to, but whatever it is, I prefer not to face it half-naked.

"Sealed it from anyone overhearing us or barging in. You'll have to trust me, Narah."

"Are you crazy?" I force a laugh. "Are you even listening to yourself? Tell me what you want, or more like, what Lyra wants." A low, rhythmic thud pulses in my temples with a mounting headache.

She pinches her lips, and I notice the nervous twitch in her jaw. What is she scared of? This girl carries power, so there is no reason for her to fear the wolves.

"You're right. I am here as commanded by Lyra. You don't know me, but I know your sister, Kaira. I cared for her when she first arrived at the coven. She was a lost girl, terrified, and calling for you and Jae."

My strength wavers, hearing the terror Kaira must have faced after we ran from the Storm Wolves pack.

"Lyra found her being attacked by two rogue wolf Alphas near our woods." She pauses as though speaking about it hurts her, but she never glances away. There is strength in her eyes as if she's seen enough ugliness in this world and has learned to numb herself from the pain. "They left her in a bad way, Narah. If it wasn't for Lyra, she'd be dead now. She saved your sister and brought her to our coven."

I can't find the words to say anything because my mind is having trouble processing what I just heard. My head fills with images of my sister being attacked, abused, torn… I hiccup a breath, and tears well in my eyes.

"D-Did they rape her?" I ask softly, the words like barbed wire in my throat.

She shakes her head. "No, but they cut her and stripped her. Lyra found her just in time."

Trembling, I wish this was just a horrible nightmare. My legs soften beneath me, and I fall to the floor on my knees. I can't get the image out of my head of how scared she would have been, how I couldn't save her from that trauma.

Piper is saying something, and I realize I haven't been listening as I struggled to pull myself back together.

"I'm sorry," she says suddenly. "I spent a lot of time with her, helping her heal, and she talked about you and Jae a lot."

"Yet Lyra spelled her to hold her prisoner," I say angrily.

Piper doesn't respond right away.

"I did everything to help Kaira, but at the coven, I'm always watched. Lyra knows your sister has powerful magic in her veins, the kind that scares her."

I blink up at her. "What does she want from us?" Anger stews in my gut. Our lives are broken and stained because everyone wants something from us. We're possessions to the wolves, a means of power to the witches. Even my parents lied to us.

"She wants you all dead, stupid girl," she snaps as if I should have known. "Lyra insists you are all a different kind of witch. The reason she released you from the coven was she needed to find your mother to destroy her, too."

A shiver passes over my skin. I'm drowning in news that shouldn't surprise me, yet it buries me under its weight. Pushing to my feet, I step away from her.

"I know Martell killed your mother," she admits. "Lyra doesn't know yet."

She'll find out soon. I turn on my heels to face her.

"Why are you telling me this? To make yourself feel better when you hand us over? If you're going to do something, just do it already," I demand, fighting the panic trying to swallow me but losing.

She gives me a strange expression, and her face pales.

"You have no idea how much trouble I'm going to be in." She's playing with her hands, twisting them over one another. "My mission here is to pretend to cast a protection spell around the Storm Wolves' camp from the undead migrating north. It's their apparent reward for their allegiance to Lyra. Except, in truth, there is no spell that can actually do this. But the wolves don't need to know this."

What does she expect me to say?

"I'm not going to report you to Lyra," she finally says, breaking the silence.

"Why? What do you get out of it?"

"It's my only chance to escape the coven."

I eye her carefully, paying attention to her fearful expression.

"You're running from the coven? What about Lyra and—"

"Fuck Lyra. There are more important things in life." She settles a hand over her stomach, rubbing it softly, and I see the small bump she's carrying. "I'm–"

"You're pregnant?" I don't give her the chance to say it. The only pregnant females I've seen are those owned by Alphas, bred, and kept under close supervision. They nest in preparation for the birth, guarded by the men.

"The father is a wolf shifter," she mutters. "I met him on a mission that never should have happened. I barely knew the damn idiot, but he gave me something I cherish, and he promised to help raise our baby. If I stay with the coven, Lyra will have the child killed. Anything tainting pure witch blood is destroyed." She shakes her head, her chin quivering. "I won't give her a chance."

"I'm sorry." I step forward, but she backs away from me.

"I'm not seeking your pity. I'm offering you a chance to escape because I like your sister. Just promise me you'll get her out from under Lyra's spell before it's too late. She won't last much longer."

"Of course." I stand steadfast, even as my head sways.

"Lyra will go ballistic when she hears you escaped Martell's clutches, and when Martell finds out his pack isn't protected from the zombies, he'll turn on the witches. Let them fight it out. More time for me to get the fuck away from the war coming to Savage Sector."

Can I blame her? I'd do anything for my sisters, just as she would for her unborn child. We might be enemies, but our desperation to survive benefits us both.

"You need to leave. We've wasted enough time. You have to run faster than you've ever have before."

"Okay, how do we do this?" I'm ready to get out of here, to find my sisters, to track down Ragnar and his men—to survive.

"There will be an explosion near this building. When that happens, run out of here, understand? Don't stop, just get the hell away from the wolves."

"Understood," I murmur as panic spreads through my chest, reminding me of what's at stake if this fails.

Piper nods curtly and crosses the room in long strides toward the door.

"Thank you," I call out.

She glances at me over her shoulder. "I'm doing this for me, and you're benefiting."

"I know," I say reluctantly. "Thank you for helping Kaira."

She gives me a tight smile, then removes the spell from the door before leaving me locked in the basement.

I pace, trying to process what she said. Pushing back the fear, I have to believe this is real and not a sick joke.

I have no power.

My mother is dead.

Ragnar and his men will have no clue where I am.

I'm pretty much in the worst possible situation and holding on to the hope that Piper's offer is genuine.

Boom!

The force of the sudden explosion seizes me, throwing me off my feet, and I fall over onto my side. The room shakes, dust raining down. Curling in on myself on the floor, my hands covering my head. Shit! Piper wasn't kidding around.

Boom!

Everything shudders harder, and one of the walls in the basement crashes down, taking part of the ceiling with it.

Screaming, I scramble away from the massive plume of dust, but I suck it in and choke on it. I cover my mouth and nose as the dust stings with each breath, but light pours in through the cloud of dust, offering me hope.

This is my chance to escape before I'm buried alive.

The building creaks and groans. It won't stay up much longer. I get up and lunge forward, frantically scrambling over the fallen wall and broken stones. My eyes tear up from the dust. By some sheer miracle, I stumble outside, and pack members are darting wildly everywhere. It takes me seconds to get my bearings, to know exactly where I am in the pack compound.

I swing left and sprint away from the chaos. Running blindly through a vegetable garden, I eye the metal fence ahead—my salvation. My heart pounds louder.

Glancing over my shoulder, pack members are scrambling while others are screaming. No one notices me, so I run for my life to escape through the gap in the fence—the same one I used to leave the pack the first night.

Under my breath, I vow the next time I see Martell, I will destroy him.

4

NIKOS

“**T**his is fucked up,” I growl, fisting my hands.

Ragnar scowls at the zombie. We all watched him transform from undead to... whatever the fuck he is now. Semi-dead? Is that even a thing? On top of that, he might be Narah's dad, which does my head in.

“Shit, man, this is so messed up.”

I cut my gaze to Stone, who strolls over to the man sitting on the couch. He crouches in front of the undead guy, wearing his stoic expression. He's always the logical one of the four of us.

“My name is Stone. Now, what did you just drink from the vial? A spell to bring you back to life?”

I roll my eyes. "Are you blind? He's still dead. Look at him."

"Nikos has a point." Crius eyes the man who might have filled out and gained color to his skin, but there's only so much repair and patching up on a corpse to pass it as the living. Whatever magic Allie used wasn't strong enough to do a complete job. One side of his face sags, his skin has patches of flesh from his arms are missing, revealing only rotted brown flesh, and he only has one ear.

Clenching his jaw, Stone glares in my direction with a *shut-the-fuck-up* expression.

"I'm not alive," the man says matter-of-factly. "I know I don't have a beating heart, and I only retain patches of my memories. Allie told me these things. She feeds me potions to reverse the virus in my body, but I can never be a complete human again." He smiles awkwardly, all teeth and creepy, but there's a vulnerability that fills me with pity. Ignoring my mind's voice is hard when I see Narah in his face. They have similar facial bone structures.

Picturing her falling apart when she sees her father this way, my gut hardens at the thought of how much it will hurt her.

"Allie fed him the energy she stole from us," Crius gripes. "We died for him."

The man pushes up from the sofa and goes to Allie on the rug, picking her up and laying her in front of the fire. "She's always cold," he mumbles.

There is tenderness in his movement as though this man with no life has feelings. He stares down at her body for a long pause before brushing strands of hair off her face. Blood from her torn throat spills onto the rug, but the zombie doesn't bat an eye. There is no feeding frenzy.

It's a joke just thinking about it.

The zombie straightens his posture and turns to Crius.

"Thanks for your donation."

We watch incredulously as he lumbers past us and makes his way into the kitchen across the open room.

"Donation? Right!" Crius mumbles. "She *stole* the energy from us for him."

"For her husband," Stone reminds him. "Anyway, why complain? What are you going to do? Take it back?"

Crius considers it for a moment.

The zombie in the kitchen makes a racket—banging cabinet doors, throwing pots, opening drawers—searching for something.

"Has he lost his mind?" Crius states. "Oh wait, he doesn't have one." He chuckles to himself.

Ragnar strides over to the guy, and I'm on his heels, leaving Stone and Crius behind to discuss their theories of the undead man.

"I can't find it," he murmurs, tossing plates, herbs, and anything on the counter in his way.

"What are you searching for?" Ragnar asks, standing feet from the man. I'm close in case things turn sour.

"I drank it all," he mutters, his brows pinched together. "When hunger takes me, it suffocates me, and I didn't think I'd need some for Allie."

"So, she has more of the potion in the house?" Stepping forward, I'm ready to tear up the damn kitchen to find it. Then I can bring Allie back, and she can explain what the fuck's going on.

The man shrugs. "I hope."

"I'm Ragnar," my Alpha states. "And you are?"

"Gregory," he whines, his brow furrowing. For the first time, I see the monster behind his eyes, the emptiness, the hunger staring at us.

I tense, ready for a fight.

With a shake of his head, Gregory's hollow expression vanishes. The monster still lives in him, but whatever Allie placed in her potion suppresses it. I see it now.

"After a few days, I'll lose control, but I promised to help Allie find her daughters." He pats his pockets, then shoves his hand into the pocket in his pants and pulls out another, smaller vial filled with more blood.

"Is that more of it there?" I ask.

"Thank goodness I didn't break it. It's for Allie's cursed daughter to drink to remove the witches' curse. Allie would be very angry if I had broken it." He hands it to me. "You better hold onto it for me."

He breaks into another twitching fit and throws himself into frantically searching the kitchen again, breaking the pantry door off its hinges and tossing it aside. The guy has strength, which worries me. Then he pauses and looks our way while holding a long ceramic plate. Is he going to hurl it at us?

I tuck the vial in my pocket, figuring that will come in very handy to know we have a cure for Kaira.

"Gregory," Ragnar says louder to grab the man's attention. "You lived with the Storm Wolves pack. Do you know where they're located?"

The man hurls a saucepan past my head, missing me by inches.

"Fuck!"

"Of course, I do," Gregory finally bites back. "Allie and I used to live there." He pauses from destroying the kitchen, lost in his own thoughts, his eyes rolling back. "Allie and I used to be so happy there."

"And your daughters?" I ask, finding it strange he hasn't yet mentioned his three girls.

He lowers his eyes to me, blinking as though he's searching for lost memories, then shakes his head. "I don't remember."

I hear the absence of emotions in his voice. Next thing I know, he moves back into the pantry, tossing containers that break and dried beans spill across the floor.

I exchange looks with Ragnar. He's batshit crazy.

"He knows where the wolves are. We force him to talk, then leave tonight for Narah," I say.

"I'll get him talking, but Gregory has me thinking. Allie performed powerful spells, meaning she might have other curses in the house we could use against the wolves, even against other witches. Take Crius and search the house, see what you can find."

I groan, wanting to get the heck out of this shithole. There's magic in the air, and I hate not knowing what I'm dealing with, but Ragnar is also a man I trust with my life. His instincts are usually spot on, so I nod and march back to the other two.

"Crius, you're with me. Stone, you have Ragnar's back."

With Crius on my heels, we step into a dark hallway that leads us past several doors. The wooden walls are worn, the floorboards creaking under our footfalls.

"We've been delegated to house searching, I'm guessing." Crius cracks his knuckles.

"Ragnar thinks we might find spells to use, and the zombie says he knows where the Storm Wolves live."

Crius halts, gawking at me. "You better not be shitting me."

I exhale loudly and turn to him. "Why would I lie about that?" I pull back my shoulders, where a sharp pain digs, where I keep my stress. Ever since we were tricked into dying, I've been tense as hell.

Crius gives me a deadpan expression. "Because you never tell us the whole truth. You hide things from us."

I frown. "Where the fuck is this coming from?"

"Don't get your panties in a twist. Since you moved in with Ragnar's pack, you've acted like the odd asshole out and kept to yourself. Even on this mission, you're behaving like a lone wolf."

"Stop talking crap," I bark and push him into the first room, his words irritating me to no end. Inspecting the bedroom, then the other rooms, we find nothing remotely resembling objects used for spell casting.

"Stone thinks so, too," Crius keeps harping, and it's pissing me off.

"So, if you have an issue with me, just say it." I move to stand in his face, heaving for breath. My fuse is about to detonate. After everything we just went through, I'm fuming and need to smash my fist through something— even if it's Crius' face.

"Nikos, we aren't the enemy." He shrugs and smiles cruelly, enjoying taunting me. "The real assholes are your family for giving you away. We're your family now, and I'm just saying to embrace it."

My fists ball—I'm going to break his face.

"What the fuck does any of this have to do with what's going on now?"

His lips thin, and I see I've finally gotten through to him.

"Because of Narah," he barks.

"What? You're making no sense."

He marches over to the last door and opens it to a set of stairs leading to the basement. It's dark as shit in there, and when I join him, a waft of putrid smells hits me, distracting me from the anger raging in my head. My skin itches, and instinct screams to get the hell out, but I know we're going down there, no matter what.

"It smells like death," I murmur.

"You think we'll find more zombies down there?"

"Or something worse," I state.

Crius flicks on the light switch, but nothing happens, and he shrugs. "Worth a try. Give me a sec." He bolts down the dark hallway into the main room, returning moments later, carrying a fire log, one end blazing with a flame.

"Let's go," he says.

I let him do the honors of entering first... just in case we're attacked.

The lower we travel, the stronger the stench. It's in my throat now, and I barely hold back my gag reflex.

"Do you even see what's been going on around us?" Crius pauses at the base of the steps, where I join him.

"Are we talking about the house, or are you still on a deranged tangent?"

"It's Narah," he barks with emotion in his voice, I've never heard before. "We all want her, man. Ragnar lost his shit when he found out she wanted us, too. I've never seen him like that... never seen him want something separate from us."

When he doesn't continue, I'm left speechless... stunned. Crius is the joker in our pack, the guy who makes light of everything to hide his dark past, and when he's not being a prick, he's killing something. He once went ballistic and butchered a small pack of rogue wolves for pissing him off.

So, this is new. It says a lot because I've felt like an outsider my whole fucking existence. I never fit in with my family or with Ragnar's parents, but this pack is the closest thing I have to feeling at home. I'm not as friendly as Crius and Stone, but that doesn't mean I don't consider them family. Far from it. I tense, thinking what I'd do if any of these men was hurt. I'd paint the world red with blood for them... for Narah.

"So, this is what you're getting up my ass for? You're worried Ragnar will make Narah pick between him and us?"

He gives a low chuff and attempts to brush it off as he casts a glance at the dark basement behind him.

My gut hardens as the reality of his ache settles in. Evidently, this has been weighing heavily on his mind to bring it up now of all times.

"She's gotten under all our skins, hasn't she?"

"Yep. I don't want her on my mind all the time, yet I can't stop thinking of her. Something's broken in me."

I chuckle and slap him on the shoulder. "Sorry to break it to you, but you were broken way before Narah came along, friend."

He arches an eyebrow. "I guess." With a grimace, he turns away, swinging the light to chase away the darkness. "Anyway, let's get this done before I hurl from how bad it stinks down here."

"Listen, Ragnar will see reason," I say, stepping deeper into the room. He has to, or he'll have three major problems on his hands. I'm not walking away from Narah, and I doubt the others will, either.

"The guy lost his cool the other day with her," I state. "When he slammed her up against the wall, I was about to jump in and tear him off her, but when they kissed, I realized there was so much more going on between them than just his words. They have shit to sort out. Hell, we all do. He has trust issues from his past fated mate. I mean, this is the first time I've seen him show any serious interest in anyone."

Crius pauses to hear me out.

"Narah isn't just another Omega to rut," I mutter. "She's special to each of us. We have to keep our unit tight, her included. She's all of ours, not just one of ours."

He coughs, then looks over his shoulder with a shrug. "You're not such a bad bloke, you know. We ought to talk more often, buddy." He goes back to scanning the basement.

"Thanks? I guess." Apparently, that's the end of the conversation, and we're now closer friends. It's the first time Crius has opened up to me about anything, so there's that.

Though I will admit, Ragnar's outburst with Narah pissed me off, and his words still roar through my mind.

For someone with no experience with men, you had no issues fucking mine. So, I'd say you know exactly what you're doing.

That was a shitty move on his part. The hurt on Narah's face stung me because we've always shared, so for him to turn on us caught me off-guard.

Moving into the darkness, I shove the thoughts aside, following the glow from Crius' torch.

"The smell stings my nostrils." Crius gags, which has my reflexes kicking in. I drag my shirt up over my mouth and nose. Taking short, shallow breaths, we hurry because I need to get out of here. "She has bodies down here. It's making me sick."

Fast footsteps move us around the room. I kick something and look down at the arm near my foot. Ice floods my veins, and I snatch the torch from Crius, who's swinging it in the wrong damn direction. "Give me that."

Sunken eye sockets, skin pulled over bones, the dead man is sprawled across the grotty cement floor. How long have they been down here?

Crius gags like he's about to hurl out his guts as I lift the torch to illuminate the rear of the room.

"Holy sweet wolf goddess."

Decayed bodies are piled on top of each other, maybe two dozen.

"Wow, Allie is a closet serial killer," Crius barks.

"Locals." I swallow the bile rising to my throat. "Don't you think it's strange they aren't zombies? Or that she drained us, but we came back to life? What about these poor suckers?"

"She drained them and didn't waste her power to resurrect them. Think about it." Crius snorts. "Then no one could accuse her of murder. I bet this would have been us at the bottom of that lake if Narah hadn't been with us."

I grimace, knowing he's right. Catching the whisper of a footstep and sensing movement behind me, I whip around to find Stone standing behind us. His eyes are huge as he's clearly seen our discovery.

"Is that what I think it is?" he asks, staring at the piles of bodies.

"She's a psychopath." Crius marches out of there. "And you guys think I'm crazy. Fuck, even this shit is beyond me."

Stone steps closer, his face pale, eyes darkening. "We can't let Narah know about this under any circumstance. It would destroy her."

I wince internally, knowing he's right, but secrets have a way of festering.

"I'm certain she knows her mother is a bitch. The woman killed us all, including her daughter, without hesitation and gave our energy to her dead husband."

"Yeah, but this takes it to a new low. Fuck, Nikos. She butchered innocent people for a man who can never be alive."

"She's doing this for more than just her husband. There has to be more to it."

"Perhaps. Anyway, Ragnar needs to see this."

"I know." Marching back upstairs, my pulse is sledgehammering at the grisly discovery. I have no issues with death when it comes with a worthy reason. I don't know Allie well enough to assume she's a complete nutcase, but I've been proven wrong in the past.

Crius and Ragnar are already chatting, and by the grim look on Ragnar's face, he knows. They march downstairs past us, and something cold presses in my veins, knowing this news will destroy Narah. To find out your mother was butchering people is not something to take lightly.

Stone marches to the kitchen, where Gregory is still flinging things around. The guy has no brains, so why would Allie kill people for him to come back to her? I shake my head.

Heavy footsteps move in the hallway, Ragnar and Crius returning. Ragnar's expression darkens, and when he stares at Gregory, then back at us, the same confusion crosses his face.

"There is no way Allie butchered all those people only for him to be in that state."

Across the room, Gregory wrenches the broken pantry door into his arms and slams it into the wall, growling with frustration.

"Guy's losing his shit," Crius murmurs and smiles; he's enjoying the show.

"There's more to this," Ragnar states, and we all migrate to stand in front of the fireplace. "He told us Allie was using him to break into the witch's compound. Whatever she gave him to drink has given him the ability to command zombies. The dead listen to him."

"No fucking way." My gaze shifts from the man still going apeshit on the kitchen, then back to Ragnar. "Okay, guess that explains the dead in the basement. So, what was her plan? Unleash the zombies on the coven and destroy them?"

"It's a damn good strategy," Stone murmurs. "Think about it. Gregory's been dead for years, right? So, she's been mastering her potion for a long time, and I bet she's left a trail of dead bodies everywhere she's gone."

"This gives us a new direction." Ragnar runs a hand through his hair, staring into the crackling fire. "I have the location for the Storm Wolves, so that's our first point of call. We're going to save Narah. After that, we'll drop her off with Jae, then we're off to kill us some witches."

"What about him?" I ask, pointing my chin at Gregory. "Don't tell me we're dragging him along?"

Ragnar shakes his head. "We'll lure him to meet us near the witch's woods in a couple nights with the promise of Allie's potion."

"Okay, so we have a new plan." Stone claps his hands in a gesture of readiness. "Let's do this."

"I'm heading out to find us horses," Ragnar states. "Find a way to calm him down. Also, see if you can salvage some food from the kitchen for our trip."

I want to roll my eyes when Crius throws himself on the couch, closing his eyes to crash, and Stone follows Ragnar out the front door.

"Great."

"Have fun," Crius mocks.

"Thanks, asshole. By the way, I hope you enjoy lying on a zombie couch where a dead man has been sleeping and bleeding."

He jerks to his feet in an instant.

I chuckle, moving into the kitchen, my thoughts consumed with the urgency to collect Narah. For Martell's sake, he better hope she hasn't been harmed. Otherwise, I'll tear him limb from limb.

5

STONE

Murder flares in my mind.

Savage. Furious. Untameable. As do all the creative ways, I'm going to kill Martell. Hang him by his cock. Skin him alive. Feed him to the undead, one bit at a time as he watches. Even then, it won't be enough for what he's done to Narah.

He's stolen her from us.

Claimed stake over Savage Sector with the witches' influence.

I hate the notion of him being her fated mate, of touching her, even speaking with her.

Fucking bastard has declared war.

The douchebag has no idea what's coming his way.

The four of us race through the field like the horseman of the apocalypse, and we're about to rain hell down on his pack. Hooves pounding the earth, we've been riding our horses for most of the night and half a day. We stopped here and there, but we're not moving fast enough for my liking.

Narah's in danger and needs us.

I'm not the kind of person who obsesses over things. Not like Crius, who gets hung up on things and can't shake them off.

Then again, I'd never met anyone like Narah, who burst into my life like a hurricane, destroying everything I believed. We faced hell together, and she's become everything to me. An Omega who dominates my thoughts, who's etched herself into my body. When I close my eyes, I can smell her honeyed scent, hear her laugh, and taste her on my tongue.

There's no denying what's happened to me.

She's my perfect little obsession. Something I've fought to tame, telling myself once I fucked her, I'd get it out of my system.

Shit, that backfired and shot me straight in the fucking heart and cock. After tasting her, my world spiraled out of control. Now, I'm drowning in desperation to find her, to fuck her brains out, to wrap her up in my arms so no one will ever hurt her again.

The four of us charge forward, barely saying a word while we ride. Nothing exists except saving Narah. Ragnar leads the charge as we follow worn paths for the sake of the horses, but we'll also need to rest again soon to not wear them into the ground. The woods are thick around us, which makes it easier for us to be ambushed. Out in the field, we could see anyone before they attacked. Here, we're at risk, especially with the undead now lurking in this sector.

"We'll rest up ahead," Ragnar calls out over his shoulder, pointing to something in the distance.

I'm at the rear of our charge and can't see shit in the distance.

Racing forward, it isn't long before we emerge from the woods into a small clearing drenched in sunlight. The guys are moving their horses toward a small creek when a scream rings through the air. A faint cry for help that's all-female.

My heart slams into my ribcage, and my mind is going at a million miles an hour at what I'd heard. I leap off my horse and run toward the sound. I don't know if the other guys heard it, but I'm seeing red fury.

"Stone," Crius yells out after me.

Something in me bellows to keep running, to follow my instinct. I'm on high alert, praying it's Narah but also scared I'll find her close to death—broken. The panicky side of my brain doesn't help, trying to slow me down, but I push forward, crushing shrubs as my ears prick to hear the sound again.

Sniffing the air, I pick up the scent of wolves. Male. Alphas.

Not waiting, I bulldoze back into the woods, where the scent takes me. Right now, I only have one mission.

Narah.

Sprinting forward, I duck low branches and weave around trees. When another cry comes from my left, I pivot sharply in that direction. I see shadows shifting in the distance, maybe three figures, hard to tell, but I bullet toward them, my mind going crazy.

My heart is ready to burst out of my chest.

I careen around a large tree, skidding across the foliage, and come to a dead stop. A growl hangs heavy in my throat at the image before me as my gaze roams the sight of three men crouching over someone.

"Get out here, asshole," one of the men barks at me.

I'm lost when she turns to me. Bright amber eyes find me, a whimper on her lips.

I can see Narah clearly on the ground, her back pressed to a tree, terror bursting from her teary eyes.

"Stone." Crying, she frantically reaches out for me.

Finding her has the world turning back into place for me, the universe back on its axis, and my hollow emptiness flooding with life. I hadn't realized how much I'd shriveled away from the fear that I'd lost her, that she'd been taken from me. Such an obsession is a cruel thing to experience. It turned me into a monster, and the constant agony I'd lose her thudded in my chest like thunder.

"You're safe now," I say to the woman who's my everything, my dreams, my future, *mine*.

"Did you hear me?" another guy snaps, shoving a fist into my arm, distracting me. "Piss off."

Snapping around, fury blinds me. I left reasonably long ago, somewhere in the mountains. All that echoes in me now is my beast. Rage burns me alive as I watch as these fucking weasels turn their attention to me. I'm going to destroy them and will fucking love it.

Heaving for breath, my wolf shoves forward, except that's too easy. No, I want to use my hands to feel every strike. I'll make them scream, to beg, to grovel. Except it's too late. I can barely feel my body now, riding high on the adrenaline to break them. Knowing that I have the power to destroy them, the ability of a god to take life sends me into a frenzy.

A howl bursts from my mouth, seeing nothing but carnage. I'm seething that these pieces of shit think they have a right to touch my Narah. Completely losing my shit, I lunge at them.

Blood. Screams. Snapped bones.

I see nothing but the three faces that I will demolish. Fists, teeth, fury. I give it all and take everything from them. Blood fills my mouth, and I spit out a piece of flesh as snarls erupt from my mouth. I will rip these Alphas apart.

I can't think, can't remember, can't stop.

Images of Narah's face, her tears give way to my madness.

I grab a sucker by the shirt and slam a fist into his face, over and over, then lift him over my head and hurl him at another guy. A punch strikes my back, and I snarl with fury. Pivoting on my heel, I kick the bastard in the gut. If I had my magic, I would have finished off these bastards already, but in truth, I don't want the easy way out. I want to crush these rogue wolf shifters with my bare hands.

I rush after him to finish this. His groans and cries are white noise, and it's irritating me. Grabbing him by the throat, I rip it out with my bare hand. Blood splatters across my face, and I sneer. Throwing myself at the other two, I dance with their death. One of them is changing into his wolf but stands no chance against me. I hurl myself at him, taking him mid-change, slamming into him until there's nothing but a broken body left.

Whipping back around to the third asshole, he's clutching the ear I ripped off him with my teeth. As they say—more like I say—there's no rest for the deplorable, so I attack, finishing him. Having him share my breathing space is not acceptable. His limp body drops to my feet.

I swing around, heaving for breath, and a sharp snarl rips from my lungs when I don't find Narah near the tree. Movement from the woods ahead reveals she's cradled in Ragnar's arms, Nikos and Crius crowding close, holding onto her, captivated by her. While I breathe easier that she's safe, a pang of jealousy strikes at not getting her in my arms first.

When they turn in my direction, there's no shock at the three assholes I just eliminated, and I shouldn't expect any. That's how our pack works.

We kill to keep each other safe, no judgment, just expect we'll do whatever it takes.

The shattering sensation that I almost lost Narah slips into the darkest recesses of my mind, and I step over the bodies to reach them.

"Thanks for leaving some action for us," Crius mutters, except with the way he's studying Narah, I'm not sure if he's more pissed I took all the kills or that she's not in his arms instead of Ragnar's.

"You were amazing and a little terrifying," she says, grinning at me. Pulling at the ripped fabric that's slipped down her shoulder, she breaks from Ragnar's arms. Her face is dirty, those huge eyes glistening with remnants of tears. "I thought I was going to die."

She rushes toward me and slams into me despite my being covered in blood. Her small arms coil around my chest as I bring mine across her back, then kiss the top of her head, wishing I could push her into my body, so no one could reach her ever again.

"I heard your cry," I explain. "There's no way I'd let you die, beautiful."

Ragnar pats me on the shoulder, then squeezes. "You heard something the three of us didn't, so amazing work." There's genuine appreciation on his face.

After the shit that went down in the mountains with him and Narah, part of me wasn't sure what to expect, but for now, things are calm between us. What comes later, we'll deal with then.

I look down at my girl. "So, guessing you escaped Martell."

"You know me." Her lips pinch to the side in a lopsided grin. "Nothing will hold me locked up for long."

"Well, I'm glad you're safe now." Nikos stands super close, his gaze meeting hers. "I really had my hopes high on finally meeting Martell."

"Get in line," Crius barks with a laugh. "He's mine, and you can have the scraps."

"I never thought I'd enjoy anyone arguing so much about who gets to kill my ex-fated mate." She wipes the blood from her cheek, and I hold her tighter. "I still can't believe you're here," she murmurs. With the way she looks up at me, then to the other guys, in her eyes, I see the terror she must have felt.

"Why didn't you use your magic against them, sweetheart?" Ragnar asks.

She twists in my arms to face the group, and I hold her against me, not ready to release her. When she raises her hands, I take several moments to understand what we're looking at.

"The black is gone from your fingers," Ragnar says, reaching over and taking her hands, studying them. "How?"

"Apparently, with my mother's cleansing of our curse, it reset things inside me. Including my magic, which I can no longer access." The ache in her voice stabs through me. Come to think of it, I haven't felt the spark of magic in my veins since the incident. With a deep inhale and a call to my power, I concentrate...but I feel nothing. Not a single thread of magic.

Fuck.

I look at Narah, who watches me. "I don't have my powers either. I can't feel them."

The edges of her mouth downturn. "I'm so sorry, Stone. I think my mother drew a lot of *our* magic into her." Instead of anger, there's only bitterness and sorrow in her words. Being mad at a dead person is never simple, says me who's internally fuming that she stripped me of my magic too.

Mother told me magic can never be taken away. It will always be inside you, even if dormant, so perhaps it's time that we need for our abilities to grow in strength once more? It better work or I'll be losing my shit because my magic comes from my mother's bloodline. A connection I never want to lose.

"I'm sorry for your loss. We've placed your mother safely in her home, so we can return to bury her," Ragnar says, then takes her hand and pulls her from my arms.

I hold back the growl in my throat at discovering my power is gone and knowing we're all shaken by how close we came to losing her.

"Let's get you cleaned up by the river, then get moving," Ragnar says. "We're not safe out here." He lifts his head, and our gazes clash. Then he smiles his gratitude, giving me a knowing nod of how much this means to him, but I did it for all of us, for me, not just him.

My wolf growls in my chest that she's mine—all mine. As Ragnar walks her out of the woods, I notice Crius and Nikos also watch her just as possessively.

"We need to talk," he tells her, something that has me following them closely, as do the other two, needing to know where everything stands between us.

Don't get me wrong. It's crystal clear in my head. She will continue to be mine, regardless of what Ragnar decides. How things between us play out all comes down to him now.

"Maybe not now," she says softly. "I want to check on Jae, and I want to stop feeling like I'm constantly scared and running for my life. I'm exhausted."

"We'll take care of you, Narah." He wraps an arm around her waist, drawing her to his side.

I keep silent for now. This time isn't about me. It's about what *she* needs.

We all make our way to the creek, where we left the horses, and I know it's going to be a long ride back.

6

NARAH

"Narah." Someone shakes my arm, and I pull away. It takes seconds for my thoughts to catch up to me, to wake up and remember where the hell I am. My brain is sluggish.

I slip open my eyes, and my vision blurs, the world slightly tilting around me. It's dark outside, and I glance down from the horse I'm still on top of. We've stopped, and I'm still hugging Ragnar.

A rush of memories overwhelms me, coming at me like a tornado.

Martell.

The pack turning on me.

My mother... her death.

Rogue wolves attacking me.

Stone killed them, and their blood and cries had pierced the air. I cheered for Stone, wanting those assholes to suffer. If he hadn't come for me, I would be dead. I know that it makes me a horrible person to wish for someone's death, but there are some loathsome people in this world who do not deserve this life.

Rogue wolves span through the forests in Savage Sector since there's not one dominant Alpha who has taken charge of this territory. The numerous smaller packs are vicious and will kill anyone getting too close to them... either that or they're taken out. Every other Alpha and Beta end up becoming rogue, attacking who they find, especially females to rut. Thing is, we're low in supply as men outnumber us at least ten to one.

So, having someone like Ragnar reign over this sector would benefit so many, even if it is a ginormous feat for him.

"You fell asleep," Ragnar says, patting my arm, stealing me from my thoughts.

"You slept like a log," Crius murmurs with a grin. "I've never seen anyone crash on a horse."

"I was exhausted and must have passed out." Meeting Stone's gaze as he steps toward the horse, I accept his help to dismount the charger. "I'm surprised I didn't fall off." I attempt to laugh, but it comes out raspy and strained as sleep still clings to me.

"I held on to you the whole ride." When Ragnar climbs off the dark horse, I look around and notice where we are. The open field, the gates in the distance manned by guards, and the set of stone steps that lead up to the wolf pack—where we left Jae. I perk up, excited to see my sister. I check out the men, who are still studying me, waiting for a response. "Okay, I crashed for a long time. My body needed the rest."

"I'm pretty sure we thought you were dead at one stage." Stone laughs. "Ragnar had to stop so Nikos could check your pulse."

"You did not," I rebut, shocked I slept through all that.

"Until you snored." Crius barks a laugh.

"Wow, I'm not sure now if I wanted to be saved by you lot." I stick my tongue out at them, which gains me tight smiles. I can't even express how incredible it is to be back in their company. Warmth blooms through me because I missed every one of them, more than I assumed I would.

Right now, there's something tense going between them, or maybe I'm still spaced out. The last time we were together, I had a huge argument with Ragnar, so I assume it has something to do with that.

"We need to celebrate, and my throat's dry as the desert. Let's get the horses to the stables, then I can drown in beer," Nikos says, his eyes only on me.

I struggle to believe how far we've come and how much they've grown on me. With a sexy wink my way, Crius helps Nikos round up the four animals, and they walk them into the night in the opposite direction.

Ragnar and Stone take position on either side of me as we head up to where the pack lives. Stone's fingers slide into my hand, and our fingers interlace. There's incredible warmth in his touch. I hold on to him, never wanting to let go.

"I want to see Jae first," I say, unable to keep the smile off my face. Just knowing she's safe and doing well is all I need.

"Of course," Ragnar says. There's a bit of awkwardness in the way he looks at me and the tightening of his jaw when he notices my hand joined with Stone's. He wants to say something but is holding back, though I know it'll come later. It's written on his face.

We reach the top of the stairs to the pack's homes. They spread outward in every direction, and more huts sit around the circular perimeter. There are at least fifty wooden buildings, and in the middle, a bonfire roars, crackling with embers and illuminating the darkness.

Several pack members near the flames are looking our way, and more guards are peppered around the place. Ragnar promised me the Alpha of this pack protects his females and that Jae would be safe. I have to believe that's the case, or I would never have left my sister behind. Now, I want to see her that much more.

Recognizing the guards, Stone lifts his chin toward them with a nod. Ragnar gazes over his shoulder, then back at me.

"Narah, I need to advise the Alpha of our arrival, arrange for a meal and place to sleep for us all, then we need to talk."

There's finality in his tone that he won't let this go, but there's kindness in his face. He's worried about something, which makes me uncertain.

"Okay, fine."

He turns and leaves without another word. I watch him walk away and blend into the night, hoping his anger from our last argument has been tempered.

Stone's hand in mine squeezes lightly. "You doing alright?"

I shrug. "I'm just not sure what he's thinking or really where we stand."

Stone's brow pulls together in frustration. "He's dealing with a lot of rejection from his past. He told you his fated mate rejected him, as did his own father, and after all this time, the scars haven't fully healed."

"He still has feelings for his fated mate?" The thought slips out, and I regret how jealous I sound. Especially considering I'm struggling with my own fated mate and my wolf being drawn to him.

Stone turns to face me and gives me a soft smile, his hands running up my arms.

"He struggles to trust. He once told me he could never love again, that losing a fated mate broke him and made him incapable of finding anyone else to take her place."

I can relate so much to this.

Stone leans forward. "Do you have any idea the impact you've had on each of us? How over the length of working with you on what was meant to be a straightforward mission, we've all ended up losing our heads over you? Each one of us is broken, Narah, maybe beyond repair, and for me, something about being with you helps put part of me back together."

"You aren't broken. Everyone is redeemable." I blink at him, and he just grins, not arguing my point, which tells me how much he doesn't believe me. Despite that, I find myself distracted by his smile. He has the most incredible smile that weakens my knees.

To say the past few weeks have been crazy is an understatement of how insane my life has become. Never in my wildest dreams did I expect to find myself in this situation—four men vying for my attention, and I want them to agree to share me. I yearn to hold and protect them from their past, just as they do with me. Maybe I've lost my mind, or maybe I've finally found the one thing to fill the hollowness within me.

When I look back up at Stone, he's staring at my mouth with a hunger in his eyes and doesn't hide it when I catch him.

"I missed you," he admits. "I was going ballistic, not knowing if you were safe. We all were. Ragnar would be crazy to do anything other than sweep you into his arms and accept us all in your life. Otherwise, fuck him. I'll steal you for myself."

I laugh, not used to men being so possessive of me. I'm the girl who'd lived mostly isolated from the rest of the world.

There was a time when my life was anything but exciting —routines to keep my sisters safe, to put food on the table, hoping when my time came to find a fated mate, he'd be kind and protect us. Well, that life went to hell in a handbasket.

Yes, my life is now a lot more complicated, and I'm in huge danger, but I've found something I never thought I would—a craving for real happiness with four Alphas. Except things aren't exactly smooth between us right now.

"You are ridiculously adorable when you pout." Stone's voice breaks me from my thoughts as he draws me into a walk in the opposite direction Ragnar went. "Come, let's get you to your sister. I also want to hear everything about how you outsmarted Martell and slipped away. Please tell me it involves him crying like a baby in pain."

I laugh, wishing that had been the case.

"It was more like luck. There was a witch with the Storm Wolves, and she basically helped me escape."

His gaze narrows. "What did she want in exchange?"

"She felt bad about how horribly the High Priestess had treated my sister, and well, I was in the right place to help her leave the coven. So, it benefited both of us." Relaying a short rendition of what happened, his eyes were glued to me. His attention falls to my chest, and with the way his brows pull together, I know he's not staring at my breasts.

"He did this to you, didn't he?" His thumb gently runs beneath the cuts Martell had inflicted, and I nod, the injuries still tender. His gaze darkens, and his shoulders stiffen. "I'm going to murder him for touching you. Fuck, I'm so sorry we didn't find you quick enough." He holds my hand tighter and with his other arm, drags me toward him with obviously no intention of ever letting me go.

"Main thing is I got away. He's more psychotic than I thought, but I didn't really know him. What I felt for him…still feel for him, is only animalistic instinct." I sigh. "I hate that I'm tied to such a monster and crave him when I would die before letting him touch me. Tell me that's not messed up."

"You want fucked up? Welcome to our pack. You're the perfect fit for us."

Something about those words, about me fitting in, floods me with warmth. I've only belonged with my sisters, nowhere else, so the smile that touches my lips overwhelms me with a strange happiness. Have I actually found where I truly belong?

Stone just grins at me and wraps his arm around my waist. "How about I show you how good I am at reminding you how perfect you are for us?" His hands dip down over my ass, and it amazes me how quickly my body burns up.

My wolf, on the other hand, snarls in protest. She and my body are at odds, and it's exhausting, but I won't become a slave to her instincts—not anymore.

I reach up on my tippy toes and place a kiss on Stone's lips. "Behave."

Except that action triggers him. Growling, he presses one hand into my back, the other threading through my hair. "Fuck, Narah," he curses against my mouth, looking ready to claim me. "You are going to kill me if I don't fuck you right away." The hard, thick ridge in his pants hardens as he rubs my back in small circles, his hand fisting my hair and holding me in place for the taking.

I missed this possessive side of him. Things have been getting wilder between us, especially considering the last time we fucked was in this very town. Now, he's driving me crazy with the way he holds me, tempting me to lose control.

Movement from my right has me noticing a local in the distance, walking past two homes, watching us.

"Uhm, it's probably not a good time," I whisper against the seam of his lips.

"Your sister is sleeping," he says, clearly thinking I'm referring to Jae. "All the lights are off in the home where she was staying." He glances at the hut several feet away, where night swallows the property. Not a single light is on, but what about others who are outside?

"I need you now," he purrs seductively.

Is it selfish of me to even contemplate this or more selfish to consider waking up the whole family so I can tell Jae I'm back?

My lips pinch as I glance up at Stone. This is definitely a huge progressive step for us, openly talking about having sex and being touchy-feely. Everything about him has my stomach fluttering. Perhaps being kidnapped by Martell has changed the dynamics between us.

"Just you and me, sweetheart." He kisses me, slowly and passionately, the kind of kiss that makes me float and rips the world out from under me. It leaves me vulnerable and remembering why I'm so heavily drawn to him. Damn him, I don't think I can ever do without such a kiss again. It's sweet, firm, and all-consuming, taking me like a storm that dominates everything in its path. He holds me locked to him, our bodies flush. His tongue sweeps into my mouth, the gesture possessive.

Hearing the creak of door hinges, we turn our heads just as a man in his late forties emerges from the home where Jae's staying. I pull from Stone, who grabs my waist and draws me back to stand in front of him.

"Don't go too far, just yet," he whispers in my ear, and when I feel his huge erection cradled against my ass, I understand he's trying to conceal his bulge from the man at the front door.

"Can I help you?" the man says, blinking sleepy eyes.

"I'm Narah, Jae's sister, and I came around to see her. I know it's late. Maybe I can just take a quick peek at her?"

He studies me for a long pause, then nods. "Oh yes, sorry, I didn't recognize you at first in the dark. She's sleeping, but you can come in."

Stone's hands on my waist soften.

"If it's not too much hassle, I would love to."

"She's been talking about you non-stop." He opens his door wider to a room lit by candlelight. "Everyone's asleep, so please be quiet."

"Of course." I step forward.

"I'll be out here," Stone says, already retreating when I glance at him over my shoulder.

With a smile, I turn and hurry into the house, excited to see Jae. I hated being away from her, so I'm ecstatic she's safe. The house is cozy, with small rooms and wooden walls covered in hanging dried flowers. We move into the tight hallway to the first room, and he carefully places his lit candle on the small table just inside the room.

"She's in the cot next to the window," he whispers.

I peer into the room as the light from the candle behind me steals some of the darkness. Blinking, I stare at three small cots in a tiny room, and to the right, Jae is curled under a blanket. My heart soars, seeing her safe and sound, as are the other two girls in the room. She and Kaira are all the family I have left, and I'll do everything to give them the life they deserve.

"Narah," her voice croaks.

Making a small gushing sound, I hurry over to her, excitement pulsing through me, and kneel next to the cot. When she pushes to sit up, rubbing her eyes, I can't wait and hug her.

"I missed you, Jae," I whisper. Her body is so warm from sleep when she hugs me, practically draped over me. Then she breathes heavily. Wait... has she fallen asleep?

"Jae?"

She flinches and pulls back, moaning softly.

"That's good," she mumbles. "Did you find Mother?"

Something pinches tight in my chest as an image of our mother flashes through my mind—dead in the woods, her throat torn out by Martell's wolves. Before I left Jae here, she told me she preferred if I didn't find our mother, and I understood her worry. Sometimes, the truth was more terrifying than what our minds may conjure up.

"Let's talk about it tomorrow. It's late, and I'd hate to wake up the other girls in the room."

"Mhm." She pulls back and slides back under the blankets, her eyes already sliding shut.

"Sweet dreams, sis." I tuck her in and kiss her brow. "I'll see you in the morning."

She's breathing heavily again, so I slip out of her room.

"Thank you," I say to the man who looks half asleep. "Sorry for disturbing you. I can breathe easier now, knowing she's okay."

His gentle smile and caring eyes remind me of my father, staring at me knowingly before he gave me words of wisdom. I used to roll my eyes at him, but now I hold on to his words with dear life. They're all I have left of him.

The man clears his throat. "Just behind our house, we have a small bathhouse we share with the neighbors. There's hot running water for the showers, and my wife has some clean clothes on the shelves." He looks at me, then rubs a thumb over his own cheek.

I imitate him and find dried blood on mine, then notice how much blood is splattered on my torn dress.

"Well, thank goodness for the night, so Jae didn't see me like this." I offer him a wonky smile. "Thank you."

"Jae is a wonderful girl who just needs time to be young. She's seen too much in her time, hasn't she?" His brow furrows, and I don't take it personally.

Everything my sisters and I have been through resulted from others' actions. I nod, wishing more than anything I could take those away from her and Kaira.

"Thanks again for looking after her."

He nods and opens the front door.

Looking around as I step out into the night, Stone is nowhere to be seen. A cold wind blows past, swishing through my hair, and I decide I'll take the man's offer. I move around the house and find a smaller wooden hut and go inside, where an oil burner lights up the bathhouse. A wooden tub is on the left, an open shower on the right, and across the back are timber shelves with towels and various folded clothes. Closing the door behind me, I hurry to the shower and flip it on. It makes a clunk, and I flinch as water spurts out in small gushes. To my surprise, it's warm at my touch, and I want to cry with joy. A warm shower is precious and rare.

Stripping, I drop my dirty clothes and jump in under the spray. Hot water strikes my skin, and I moan under my breath. Grabbing the bar of soap I find on the small shelf on the wall, I scrub the blood off me, lathering every inch of my body, scrubbing all the blood off my body, then wash my hair. Finishing my speed shower, I turn off the water, not wanting to use it all up. I ring out my hair over my shoulder, realizing I didn't grab a towel from across the room. Water stings my eyes as I grope for a towel I hope is hanging on the wall just outside of the shower. No such luck. I swing around to hunt for one, and a shadow falls across me. I tense, a squeak breaking the silence when I find someone else in the room.

My eyes widen in shock.

7

NARAH

"H-How long have you been watching me?" I whine.

The corners of Ragnar's mouth lift into a sinful grin, enjoying the impact he has on me. Normally, I'd have a witty response, but right now, it's stuck somewhere in my libido, especially since I can't control my gaze from wandering over his spectacular body.

"Long enough."

Completely naked, casually standing feet from me, his head tilts to the side, and his lips part as he takes in a sharp breath at my nudity. By the looks of his erection, he's been having a good time watching.

I gasp as I feel heat climb through me, curling around and swallowing me. My hands snap over my body, more out of instinct since this man has seen me naked before, and I'm torn between running to grab a towel and letting him stare all he wants.

Says me, who can't keep my eyes off him—a chest carved out of stone, abs all angles and curves.

His bicep flexes as he runs a hand through his hair, and butterflies burst through my stomach the longer I stare at this beautiful man.

He's perfection—tall, broad, and lust gazing behind his eyes.

My attention lowers down his body once more because I have no self-control. His cock is hard, sitting upright, and the long vein that runs its length bulges. Of course, he's huge, yet seeing it again reminds me of the anaconda I'm dealing with.

His hand dips lower, following my stare, and wraps around his thick cock. He palms it and hisses, making his intentions for me clear.

I might have just moaned and squeezed my legs together at the sight.

"Wh-What are you doing here? How did you know I was here?" I say all in one breath, surprised I can even form words.

All my rational thoughts vanish, losing myself too fast, especially under his gaze. I love the way he stares at my body, even if it scares me that I'm not good enough compared to his fated mate. I can't get Stone's words out of my head about Ragnar's struggles to forget her. In my mind, she's extravagant and a sex goddess. I tell myself his connection to her comes from their wolves but try telling that to the green-eyed monster inside me that wants to claw her face off.

"I followed you in here to talk, but then..." He runs the back of his hand across his mouth in a gesture that implies he's drooling. "I forgot what we were going to talk about."

My body tightens, hyper-aware of every move he makes as he strolls toward me, his cock bouncing with each step, hypnotizing me. I never thought I'd be drawn to such a huge cock.

"Make yourself busy and grab me a towel," I state, putting more sass in my voice, figuring if he comes any closer, I'll lose all control.

He keeps his eyes on me and stops right in front of me. *Oh my, did his cock just touch my stomach?* I might have gasped.

"You won't need one," he rasps, his voice gravelly and so sexy. Taking my hands, he lowers them from across my body. "Don't hide your body from me. It's so beautiful, and I want to see every inch of you."

My body thumps with arousal, his heat enveloping me, and that devastatingly sensual smirk completely undoes me. Even my wolf, who's been betraying me with Martell, silences as though she knows a *real* Alpha stands in our presence.

Ragnar lifts my hand and presses the tip of each finger to the soft cushion of his lips, then kisses them. He studies my body, my face, all of me. My cheeks are warm, and my pulse races in my ears. With him, I feel incredible and invincible, as if I am allowed to be adored, as though I mean the world to him.

"What did you want to talk about?" I ask meekly while the pulse between my legs throbs. I yearn to lean in and feel his lips against mine, to feel every inch of him on me.

"All I can think about is how I'm going to fuck you up against the walls, how your screams will tell everyone you're mine." His hand slides down to my shoulder. "Do you know how hard it was watching you run your hands across your gorgeous little body in the shower and not join you? How much I want to sink my cock into you."

I'm stunned at his admission, though I really shouldn't be. Since I escaped from the Storm Wolves, I've noticed the struggle in the men's eyes when they stare at me, between tension and unbearable lust.

"First," Ragnar says, drawing my attention back to him. "I want you on your knees, sucking me off," he commands, pressing down on my shoulder. "I need you to memorize my taste, to remember how my cock feels in your mouth.

Tonight, I'll imprint my mark on you again, and it's going to fucking stick." Ragnar's scorching hot words are a whisper across my lips.

With him, I never really know what to expect. Tonight, he's in a darker, teasing mood, provoking the tingle inside me that started the moment I spotted him watching me, the itch to have him claim me... all of me. Even if my wolf pined within me for Martell, twisting around my heart like barbed wire, my body demands Ragnar.

With a mind of their own, my knees soften as I lower myself in front of him, his cock in my face. He's big, thick, and long. Everything about him is impressive. I might salivate, even if I'm new at this. That hypnotic scent, a light musk, envelopes me, and his sex floods me. It's captivating.

"Does this mean you're now willing to share me with your men?" I say, confidently lifting my gaze to him.

Through hooded eyes, he looks at me, then scratches his chin.

"This has nothing to do with them," he growls, catching me off guard.

Okay, that's still playing on his mind.

"I can still smell Martell all over you, and it's driving me fucking crazy. I'll remove every inch of him from you and remind your wolf who you belong to. Tonight, I want you to submit to me." His hand slides to the back of my head and pushes me toward his cock. An incredible cock at that.

Focus, Narah. I'm struggling to think straight when I'm face-deep in his groin.

Ragnar is rougher tonight, darker, and maybe I shouldn't give in to him so easily, but looking up into his eyes, I know we both need this to patch things between us. What he offers me is pure bliss and an escape.

Curling my fingers around his shaft, I tighten my grip slightly, and he jerks in my hand, his skin on fire and full of rock-hard heat.

Suddenly nervous, I admit, "This is my first time doing this."

"Then we'll go slow." There's ruthlessness in his voice, a dominance to claim me, to make me his, and goddess forgive me, but I crave him to where my brain fogs.

Gripping his cock, I bury him in my mouth, and an excited buzz travels the length of my spine. Surprisingly, he's warm in a comforting way. He tastes slightly salty and sweet, hard to pinpoint any flavor, except to say it's extremely pleasant.

I suck him, listening to his sharp inhale, which has me tingling all over. Bopping my head up and down, I sense his body stiffening and know I'm doing it right. His hand tangles in my hair as he guides me slowly forward, pushing himself deeper into my mouth. He hits the back of my throat, which closes as my gag reflex kicks in. Pulling him out of my mouth with a pop, my eyes water. I blink up at him, gasping for air. He runs his thumb across my cheek, soothing me.

"Just take a long breath and relax, little fox. Work your throat into accepting me. Now, open up for me, and let's try again."

With his hand on my jaw, I draw him back into my mouth and close my lips around him. Working my throat around him, I gradually take more... and remember to breathe. I flatten my tongue beneath his shaft while holding on to his strong thighs.

He moans, his hand on the back of my head, and works himself deeper into me. He feels perfect in my mouth, soft but firm. I suck on him, stroking him with my tongue, and work my throat to take more of him.

"I love seeing you this way... on your knees with my cock fully in your mouth. It's such a beautiful image."

The urge to release him and make him beg me for more is tempting. His hips jerk forward, but he keeps his hand on my head. He needs to hold on to control, to dominate me, even when it comes with extreme pleasure.

As much as I'm sitting on the fence with him forcing me to remain under his command, fiery arousal pools between my thighs with my growing desire. It would be easy to walk away from him if he wasn't so sinfully gorgeous and didn't drive me crazy.

I glide one of my hands underneath his balls, pushing up and cupping them. His growls are all the consent I need to keep going as I suck and massage him.

His hand tightens on the back of my head, fisting my hair, his breathing racing. I never pause because there's something in me that seeks his approval, to know I pushed him over the edge with my actions.

"Enough," he hisses and pulls out of my mouth. Gazing up at him, I lick my lips, and he takes my arm, bringing me to my feet. His face is flushed with desire.

"Let me finish," I say, reaching for him.

He takes my hands in his. "I'm nowhere near finished with you, but tonight, I'm not going to come in your mouth. Tonight, I need you to come all over my cock." He smirks, and there's wickedness behind his eyes.

His fingers on my chin, tilting my head back, and he leans in. My heart beats quicker. Drawn to him, I move forward, lifting myself on tippy toes to reach him, and our mouths clash. I inhale a desperate breath, and he kisses me roughly. My lips will be bruised in the morning, but still, I press myself closer, holding on to his arms, longing for his touch, for him to claim me. I can't stop my body's reaction.

Taking my elbow, he draws me out of the shower and moves us to the middle of the room, where the floor isn't slippery with water. Feet from the door, he crouches in front of me, and the thought of someone walking in on us plays on my mind, and that perhaps I should find something to lock us inside.

His mouth suddenly wraps around my breast, and I forget everything. He suckles on my nipple, pulling at it until it hurts in a way that has me moaning for more. There's no pause as he follows the same assault on my other nipple sharp nips on the breast, I know would leave marks.

My hands brush through his hair and fist it as my pulse thumps louder in my ears. The wanton desire within me builds, and the sensation is intoxicating. He has me losing control as the heat pools between my legs. Taking a leaf out of Ragnar's book, I push him down my body, needing him where I'm aching.

He laughs darkly as he lowers to his knees. Scooping an arm behind my knee, he puts my leg over his shoulder, opening me up.

"Fuck! I love the way you smell. I'm going to ruin your pussy experience for anyone else, and you'll never forget me. Afterward, I'm going to fuck you up against the wall so hard, you'll still feel me a week later." He pushes his face between my legs, locating my throbbing clit.

I moan, holding onto his hair as his tongue laps across the seam of my pussy, pushing between the folds. I'm soaking wet, which he devours. Squirming against him, he ravages me, and I'm shuddering from his words, from how roughly he eats me. Ragnar's unrelenting, forcing me onto his slippery road, where I don't think I'll ever forget the things he does to me.

At that moment, my wolf whines, but I'm tired of her protests, exhausted of that pining in my body for Martell. I want it gone, and Ragnar offers me a way out.

Sucking my inner lips, he pushes two fingers inside me, thrusting so hard, I'm on the verge of losing myself. I grind myself against his face, holding on.

"Oh God, don't stop." My body shakes ferociously at how hard he fingers me.

He glances up at me, his mouth glistening.

"*I* am your god, Narah," he growls. "You'll worship me. You'll beg me for more and spread those pretty legs for me whenever I demand it."

"Ahhh," I gasp as he fingers me hard, never pausing. His grin is pure evil, knowing I am at his mercy. When he presses the flat of his tongue to my pussy, flicking my clit, my body tightens, and an avalanche of arousal crashes through me. I thrash as I come completely apart over his mouth. He buries his face against my pussy, sucking, taking it all.

I'm shaking, my legs weak, a scream streaming from my throat. He's the only thing holding me up. The sensation is mesmerizing, leaving me a complete mess, heaving for breath and my pussy pulsing. Losing track of time, I have no idea how long I've been quivering, coming down from my high, but it feels like hours, the most blissful hours of my life. Of course, it's more like minutes, but I'm smiling, glowing.

Ragnar lowers my leg from his shoulder, and I'm unstable on my feet, but his grip on my hips steadies me. His fingers press into my skin, heightening the sensation that still courses through me. He rises before me, broad and so intimidating.

"Have you ever tasted yourself, Narah?"

I shake my head. "I'm not exactly experienced with these things."

"Oh, you are doing incredibly well."

His chin and mouth shine with my cum, and there is a slight moment when I'm proud to see this powerful Alpha with my cum on his face.

"I want to taste myself on you," I purr in a husky voice.

He kisses me without ceremony, our lips dancing in their own carnal show. I taste myself on his mouth, on his tongue. It's light, almost sweet, and a bit spicy, the scent making me heady. He pushes against me, rubbing my cum all over my mouth, cheeks, and jawline.

"It's kind of sweet."

"You taste like honey, Narah, sweet nectar, and I want it all over me," he rasps, then licks his lips. Powerful hands fall to my hips, down to the back of my thighs, and I'm off my feet in seconds. Wrapping my legs around this strong man's waist, I loop my arms around his neck to hold on.

With one hand on my backside, he grips me as though I weigh nothing. His other hand slides between us and grabs his cock, sliding it across my slick and finally pushing his tip into me. I arch against him, pressing my breasts against his bare chest, feeling already how much he'll stretch me.

"Are you ready for me?" he asks as if that's even a question when I'm drenched and moaning for him.

"Good, I'll take that as a yes. I'm going to fill you with my seed and replace every molecule of Martell's scent on you. After this, there won't be anywhere you can go without me finding you."

I blink at him, breathing fast. He's a furious monster, jealous as hell that Martell was next to me. I tense, better understanding the truth of how obsessive this Alpha is. I should be annoyed and shove him away, yet I stare into his gaze, ready to give myself to him over and over.

"I'll take it all, Ragnar, just fuck me." I push the other thoughts out of my head, knowing they'll come back to haunt me later. Right now, I just want Ragnar to steal me away from this world and make me forget about Martell.

A heavy growl rumbles from his chest as he presses into me without pause, without taking time to fit inside me. I cry out, my body tensing as he drives into me to his hilt, and I'm gasping for air. Fuck me, but I feel every inch of him crammed into me, pushing against my inner walls.

The room sways as he takes me hard and fast. My fingers dig into his powerful muscles across his neck, rocking up and down on his erection as he jackhammers into me.

His eyes cast down momentarily to my bouncing breasts, then back up at me with his delicious grin. The muscles in his neck clench, holding my stare while staking his claim wildly.

In my heart, I am utterly lost to this man. I don't know when I fell so hard and became faithful to him, but I know I won't bend about picking him over the other men. It breaks me to think about it, and I need to make him see sense.

Deep down inside, I know if he doesn't agree, it will destroy me.

"I'm crazy for you, Narah," he pants.

I know he means every word, and it touches me somewhere in my chest. When I kiss him, it's addictive, and I'm hungry for him—just how he makes me.

Our tongues tangle, and I cling to him. When I come up for air, a moan spills from my lips as my body grows tight with the escalating climax peaking within me.

He pauses for a few moments as I catch my breath, then walks us toward the wall, still thrusting into me. I don't know how he's managing it, but his stamina and strength are insane. Even if he's not exactly walking straight, it's super impressive.

"I'm close," he growls, his shoulder crashing against the wall to hold himself, his whole body shaking.

"Whoa," I gasp from the impact, but he's too far gone. He roars, his explosion ripping through him. Turning his back to the door, he holds me and thrusts his hips.

Fire bursts within me as I feel him pulsing inside me. Screaming and shuddering against him, I feel him come inside me, filling me with his seed. His lips are on my neck, pinching my flesh, and his breaths grow faster.

I'm panting, my pussy soaked from his fucking. His hands slam against the door behind me, and I'm holding onto him to not fall off. He's desperate and wild, and the animalistic sounds he makes are my new addiction.

Then he bites down on my neck.

"Oh, shit," I call out, pinned in place by him. The beautiful agony of his teeth breaking skin, my body tears apart as my orgasm rips me to shreds, and another wave of carnal desires crashes over me, rocking me at my core.

I feel him growing inside me, thickening. He's knotting, ensuring he fills me to the brim, keeping me captive under his spell.

"You are mine now," he snarls, his voice and gaze darkened from how far we've fallen. Blood smears his lips... my blood.

Wood breaking sounds around us, loud and unexpected. Next thing, the door behind Ragnar gives way, ripped right off its hinges, and smacks to the ground. We fall with it, and I scream out of pure shock. Ragnar crashes, hitting the flat door with his back, with me locked to him. I bounce against his body, but he holds me tight, holding me safe.

It only takes moments for reality to check in and for us to realize we're lying outside the bathhouse on a broken door, and we're not alone. Two guards stand nearby, just as surprised as we are, their orb-like huge eyes taking in the sight.

Heat blushes across my cheeks, and I tuck myself against Ragnar, who pushes himself to a sitting position, his arms coiled around my back. He twists his head to the stunned guards.

"What the fuck are you looking at?" he bellows. "Fuck off before I rip your eyes out of your sockets."

The men scramble out of there. Even with my heart beating at a million miles an hour, when I look over at Ragnar, he gives me a wonky smirk, and I break out laughing. He growls, and his body stiffens.

"My little fox, keep constricting my dick like that, and we're going to be locked together all night long."

He's stuck inside me, his cock engorged, and right now, I have a bad case of the giggles.

"Guess that's a problem we'll have to deal with."

8

RAGNAR

I t's been over an hour since I fucked Narah, and I can still feel her.

Even as we sit outdoors on a log by the bonfire, I can't get her out of my head.

The softness of her body against mine, legs snaked around my hips, and my cock buried deep in her sweet cunt, are imprinted on me. She'd been dripping wet, and her taste and smell had invaded me. Even now, my fingers tingle with the memory of her gorgeous tits in my palms.

By the stunned look on her face, she hadn't expected me to bring her to her knees in front of me. She was beautiful, her eyes dilating, her breath catching in her throat when she looked up at me. It scared her how much she wanted me. I saw it in the way she covered herself, then greedily sucked my cock.

I liked her looking scared and defeated before me.

Fucking someone as perfect as Narah is a distraction I've permitted myself when I should have known better. When I should have taken what I wanted and not looked back.

Although did I even have a choice? I doubt it. She has a body made for sin, and every time I look at her, I want to bury my cock and stay inside her, to feel her pussy squeeze down on me. Her cries for more still suffocate me, weaken me, so how the hell am I meant to deny that?

I'm not ready to leave her side. I'd craved her since we got her back, and the first thing I did was get laid, figuring I'd get it out of my head. Of course, it did fucking nothing. Half the time, I trick myself into believing *that* shit works —get into her pants and not deal with the other shit in my head.

Now, this stunning creature watches the bonfire in front of us while the moon glows heavily across the landscape. She's enjoying a roast ham and cheese sandwich. It took two hours for my engorged cock to go down, and by the time we emerged from the bathhouse, the other guys had all gone to bed. So, I had some food quickly made for us.

Stuffing the last bite into her mouth, she brushes away the crumbs from the dress she'd found in the bathhouse. I'd have to arrange for Stone to fix the broken door in the morning. He's the handy one in our pack.

"I don't think it worked," Narah says quietly, and if I wasn't watching her, I might have missed her words.

"What's that, little fox?" I turn to face her, swinging a leg over the log, straddling it to face her.

She places her empty plate on the ground near her feet and pushes her wild, dark hair out of her face. The wind's picked up, sending the fire into a flutter and tossing embers into the air like fireflies. Narah stares at it in amazement, then glances back at me.

"What we did, you know?"

Is she blushing? Across the bonfire are several locals. After we broke the bathhouse's door, she became jumpy around the Bane Wolves in this pack.

There's something utterly enjoyable watching every movement Narah makes. She rubs the crumbs from around her mouth, and I consider leaning in and licking them off her face. Tucking her hands under her legs, she stretches out and wiggles her toes toward the blaze's warmth. Her legs are long and toned, and she's on the thinner side, something I'll need to rectify.

Perhaps I enjoy her too much, which might explain why she has me in her trance. I doubt she realizes how deeply she has her claws in me or how much further I wanted to push her during sex. I crave to see her tied up and completely at my mercy. Images of how beautiful she'd look send jolts of desire straight to my cock.

Next time for sure.

I shake my head and focus on what she said.

"You mean me fucking you?"

Her eyes widen with shock. "You gotta say it so loud? Why not scream it for everyone to hear. Geez, I bet they're already all talking about us breaking the door."

I chuckle, adoring the threads of innocence she holds on to.

"Okay, you're going to have to elaborate because I have no clue what you're talking about."

She pauses and pulls a bent leg between us as she swivels to face me, then her gaze drops.

"Your mark... I don't think it worked." Her hand raises to her neck, where my bite blushes pink on the side of her neck.

"What do you mean, didn't work? Of course, it did." My brow furrows.

She exhales loudly. "My wolf still pines for Martell. I feel her, even now, stirring within me, whining. I hate the longing that rises in me. I hate the bastard, yet my chest squeezes with grief at being so far from him. Last time you marked me, I felt the change almost instantly, but now, there's nothing there."

Her words hit me like a ton of bricks. How the hell didn't the mark stick?

I watch the way the bridge of her nose wrinkles and close the space between us, shuffling closer. With her bent leg cradled against my groin, I push the loose strands fluttering across her face, needing to fix this.

"Let me try something," I say, placing a palm against her warm chest. My wolf surges forward, just as he had earlier in the bathhouse, eager for a connection, desperate to bond. Closing my eyes, I sense her wolf's vibrations, fast and aggressive, not what I'd expect from a wolf connected to mine. I tense, not understanding what I did wrong.

"I don't understand how," I say, lowering my hand to my side. "It should have worked. My wolf called to yours."

"Ever since my mother cleansed us, I feel as if I've lost bits of myself." She swallows, then sighs. "I tell myself it'll just takes time, then I'll be back to normal, but I still don't have my magic, and my wolf is craving Martell stronger than before. Plus, I don't know how to tell Jae about our mother. I'm toying with saying we didn't find her and leave it at that. I mean, to find something you've lost, then have it stolen again is heartbreaking. I can't do that to my sister."

"That's a lot to carry on your shoulders, Narah." My chest aches, thinking about how much thought she's given to all the problems, adding to the growing burden that I still haven't told her about her father. Is that something she needs to worry about on top of everything else? If I don't tell her and she finds out, will she hate me?

"These are things you can't control, but once a witch, always a witch, Narah. I've never heard of one losing their powers."

"What if I'm the first?" The corners of her mouth deepen with worry lines.

It troubles me to see her this way. I reach over and stroke her cheek, running a thumb over her sweet lips that deserve to smile more often.

"Back home in Denmark, there are witches who carry dormant power, which activates later in life."

"How?" she asks with a hint of desperation.

"Usually, a traumatic event or being in life-threatening danger can trigger it."

"Great," she sighs and seems to sink in on herself. "Both things happened to me and still nothing. What if I'm really broken, Ragnar? What if I can never do magic again?" Her brow knits in frustration.

"You will always be my Narah. Nothing changes who you are, how you behave, and what you do. You told me most of your life, you had to hide your powers, right?"

She shrugs, then nods. "Yeah. I know what you're going to say, that I survived without it before, but that's not the point. Kaira remains with the witches, so how am I supposed to save her now with no magic?"

I straighten. "We'll find a way to bring your powers back. If one witch helped you escape Martell, we'll find others to assist us with your sister." Though I have plans to take them out without Narah knowing. In two days, Gregory will meet my men and me by the Poisonous Woods where the witches are.

The high priestess bitch dies first. Then I'll bring back Narah's sister.

If all goes well, Narah may never need to know about the grisly fact that her mother resurrected her dead father from where Narah had buried him.

She sighs again. "My mother told me I wasn't an ordinary witch. Our family line makes me a sorceress."

I tense, knowing all too well about sorceresses. I understand how dark their magic is and that they draw their energy from other people, depleting them to death. I've heard stories about them but never met one.

Worry flares in Narah's expression, and I think back to everything I'd witnessed from Narah's mother.

Draining us to death.

Dead villagers in her basement.

Her father brought back to life.

Here I assumed she used powerful potions and spells to do it, which begs the question—what was Gregory drinking from the vial that looked like blood? I have a terrible suspicion he drank Allie's blood, which would be infused with magic she siphoned from poor suckers like us. Is that why we, and the dead in the basement, didn't come back as undead? Her magic affected us differently, just as it had flatlined Narah's powers.

"I will not be like my mother," Narah says abruptly, pulling back her shoulders in a defensive move.

"I never said you would be."

"Yet you look at me as if I'm a monster." Her eyes narrow in on me.

"That's not true." I shake my head. "I look at how brave you are after everything you've been through."

"Stop bullshitting me, Ragnar. Just say it as it is. My mother was a fiend, who drained people. For all I know, she's killed a bunch of others."

Well, she's not wrong there, but I say nothing. That won't help her cope with the reality of what her mother's done.

Narah turns from me and stares into the flames, which reflect in her amber eyes. I can almost see her mind working overtime, going through every memory, trying to make sense of her missing magic. I let the silence sink between us, but it isn't long before she's twisting her head in my direction.

"I don't really want to talk about this anymore if that's okay. Anyway, you wanted to talk to me?" Her words are clipped, and she's pulling away from me.

"I did. Before the shitstorm hit us, we didn't end up on good terms."

She studies me, and I'm not sure what she expects me to say. That I'm sorry? That I'm absolutely smitten with her? That it turns me into a jealous sonofabitch, even of my own men, who are like the brothers I never had? They are family, yet I burn up when I see them flirting with her, touching her. It kills me that Stone and Nikos have fucked her, and I know Crius is vying for his chance.

I clench my jaw, torn in half by how shitty I feel.

"I've never felt this way about anyone, let alone four Alphas. I know you have some things to work through from your fated mate leaving you. Stone told me; please don't be mad at him. I opened up to him about us first." She's talking fast, sounding nervous.

"I'm not upset. They all know about my past." I'm more annoyed about her not coming to me to talk about her issues.

"Yet you don't trust them to be with me?" Her voice is soft, and there are heartfelt emotions behind her words, not accusations.

Ignoring my mind's voice that tells me Eisa, my fated mate, promised to be mine, too, I just look at Narah. She could be everything I need. Someone to replace the gaping hole in my soul I'd resigned would remain barren. But what stops her from one day deciding I'm not good enough? That one of the other guys is all she needs?

It's fucking eating me alive that I have such thoughts, and I hate myself. I'm a damn Alpha and about to bring war to the Savage Sector to claim it as my territory, yet I'm pining like a love-struck teenager that I'll get hurt.

Get your fucking head together, Ragnar.

My wolf snarls in my chest to wake me back to my senses, to see the beauty in front of me and not destroy the only chance I have with her. Sure, I'm an asshole. Part of me isn't sorry because I refuse to let anyone ruin me again, but the other part of me craves to let go of the past.

"Everyone tells me time will change me, but it's done nothing so far," I admit. "I know you want us to share you, but I'm struggling with that idea. I've shared everything with my men, but I've never met anyone like you, and selfishly, I want you all for myself."

She doesn't say a word, but her expression conveys disappointment. Her eyebrows pull together, and I regard her curiously. She cares that much about my position on this? I'm drawn to her like a moth to a flame, can't stay away if I damn try, so there's reassurance in seeing this isn't an easy situation for her either.

I clear my throat. "You're mine, Narah, but if bringing you happiness means accepting sharing you, then..." I take a deep breath that rattles all the way down to my lungs. "I'll have to find a way."

Her smile melts me. She reaches over, hugging me tightly.

Now, I know what's going to happen. I have to keep my word to Narah, and I owe it to myself to finally break away from my past and forget my fated mate, who rejected me.

Then why the fuck does it feel like I've made a mistake, and I'll never be able to walk away from this if I don't win over Narah?

9

NARAH

"I promise, they won't mind if I go fishing with them," Jae insists, sitting across from me in the pack mess hall. It's big enough to fit most of the Bane Wolves pack comfortably, though it's late morning, so there's hardly anyone there. Well, except for my sister and her new friends, plus a handful of people somewhere behind me in the room.

Without a word, she lets go of my hand and turns to her friends, who are taking their dirty dishes to the front. Throwing any waste in the bin, they place their plates with all the other dirty ones in buckets.

"The pond is on their pack land, so it's safe." Jae shrugs. "I know it's lame, but I want to go with them. They make me laugh. You can come, too." Jae looks at me, hopeful.

I can't really blame her for wanting to hang with her friends and do normal things. She missed out on so much of that. Back at Storm Wolves, for her own safety, she spent little time with other kids. Too many desperate men leered at her as if she was food, and it creeped me out. I wanted her safe.

"It's not lame at all. Sounds like fun, and I'd love to join you, but I have a few things to get done today," I say, my thoughts already pivoting toward finding Ragnar and talking to him about how we're going to rescue Kaira. No distractions or emotions like last night. I just want both my sisters with me. After that, I'm not too sure where we'll go. Getting my head screwed on right with Ragnar and his men is priority. Things are volatile, simmering as though they might explode.

"Really?" Jae jumps to her feet from the wooden bench and collects her breakfast plate from the table. "Thanks, Narah. I'll catch us something for supper." She is so giddy, bouncing on her toes, and I love seeing her like this.

"Your friends' mother is going with you, right?"

She nods. "There are several families going and all their mothers as well. I swear, it'll be safe."

"Of course, it will. I want to hear all about it when you return." A pang of guilt stirs in my chest. I'd love to join her, but I need to find the men and find out when we're going to rescue Kaira. Then, if I have time, I'll join Jae for some fishing.

She squeals and comes over to hug me, bits of egg spilling on my lap from her plate. I just laugh and wipe the mess off faded jeans as she runs to her friends.

Leaving the mess hall behind, I stroll through the sunlight. By the time Ragnar and I returned to our hut last night, the other guys were snoring like bears. I fell asleep in Ragnar's arms, and in the morning, the hut was empty. I had seen none of them since.

When I step out from behind a wooden hut, I spot Ragnar. He's half turned away from me, in close conversation with Lyssa, the pack Alpha's daughter. It takes me off-guard, especially when she winds her arm around his, and he doesn't push her away.

My eyes bore into them as fire erupts in my chest, and the truth pummels my mind. Her father threatened to give her to his men as their mate because there weren't enough females to go around. So, how much different is her monster of a father from Martell?

When Ragnar agreed to take her as his mate, it was a purely strategic decision on his part to gain this pack's support in his attempt to take over the Savage Sector, a decision made before he knew I existed, and now things are completely messed up. I can't hate the girl for trying to survive, yet I want to rip them apart.

Her blonde hair drapes loosely over her shoulders, and she's in a white dress that hits across her thighs with frills across her low neckline and short sleeves. She keeps pouting her ruby lips like a damn frog. I can't ignore how beautiful she is. High cheekbones, crystal-like eyes, and ample breasts, she rubs against Ragnar's arm. Her faint giggle fills the air at something he said, but from my angle, I can't see his face, let alone hear what they're saying.

I'm dazed and burning up with red-hot anger. My head and instincts are warring, and the only solution is to find Lyssa another man and get her the hell away from mine. A ridiculous and impossible idea, seeing I know no one in this town.

They are standing close, and I'm inches from bursting toward them. Instead, I do one better and retreat, then rush frantically around the back of the hut and come up on the other side to be closer to them. I'm desperate like that, it seems.

I dart to an apple tree that towers between two homes, dangling with heavily laden branches, red globes everywhere. They smell so sweet and heavenly, but I ignore the temptation and tuck myself behind the trunk before peering out to watch Ragnar and Lyssa.

They're feet from me, and I'm shaking all over, my insides set aflame.

"Ragnar, it will look suspicious to Father," she purrs, still pouting.

My insides burn hotter.

Ragnar looks at her dismissively, then tilts his head to the sky, releasing a sigh.

"That won't work for me."

On the bright side, he's not drooling all over her, but that doesn't stop me from holding on to the tree digging in my claws as if it was Lyssa.

"Well, you'll have to. It's not that hard to have one dinner with your mate. You've been gone from me so long, Ragnar. I miss you." She bats her eyes at him.

His nostrils flare, and he looks away, a mask of pure hatred sliding over her face.

"It's because of her, isn't it?" she snarls. "I smell her all over you. It's disgusting that you show interest in a half-breed you brought into our home. She's a mongrel."

I catch my breath. *That bitch!*

Ragnar swings back toward her with a growl, and she recoils, realizing she's pissed him off. He closes the distance between them in two steps and towers over her, heaving for breath. Arms tight by his side, I expect him to strike.

"Enough, Lyssa! Narah belongs to me, and that's not going to change."

Her grin drops, and she glares as Ragnar turns to leave once more.

"One word from me to Father, and you'll lose your allegiance with the Bane Wolves. You need to forget her."

He pauses and looks over his shoulder at her with pure hatred.

"If you do, you'll become the whore of this pack at your father's word."

Her shoulders rear back, her face pale as milk. With her chin high, her eyes flash to him with a threat.

"That's a risk I'm willing to take. Are you willing to do the same, Ragnar?"

I swallow hard, and despite my earlier words, I really hate her. Sure, desperation makes people do unforgivable things, but that's no excuse.

Expressive blue eyes narrow on Lyssa. "One meal," he grits through clenched teeth.

Shit, is he kidding me?

"Good." A smile unravels over her lips once more. "Now, Father wants to see you. Shall we go?" She's so sickly-sweet, I feel sick to my stomach.

I only see red as she sways her hips in his direction.

Stepping out from behind the tree, fury flashes in my mind. I lunge after her just as someone grabs me from behind by my waist and turns me away from them.

CRIUS

"Put me down," Narah hisses.

"Calm down," I whisper in her ear, her back flat against my chest as I swing us away from Ragnar's direction. The moment she lunged for him and Lyssa, I knew what would happen. Our witch had grown possessive of Ragnar and would have ruined months of work cultivating a relationship with the Bane Wolves.

"Let me go!" She thrusts against me.

"Hush now." I tighten my arm, locked across the front of her shoulders. "Ragnar knows he's yours and that you're powerful enough to fight for him, but not on this, my little hummingbird."

"All of you may be alright with this, but I'm not."

Her words trigger something. Ragnar means a lot to me as well, but if she keeps brushing that gorgeous ass, we're going to have a problem.

I came into this mission for Ragnar for one purpose—to help him gain his territory, so I can attain my warrior entry into Valhalla. The path is simple as fuck, and I know Ragnar hates my plan, but I agreed to join him for that sole purpose—which he accepted. You see, he has this way of making you completely loyal to him and collects followers like zombies are drawn to the living. The guy has a heart of gold, even if he's terrifying as shit when he's furious, and that's a hard quality to find in people in this damned world.

Narah isn't any less impacted by him.

I hold on to her, trying to make her settle down when I shouldn't give two fucks, yet I find myself captivated. I'm having thoughts about stripping her down and showing her what she's done to me. To let her experience a high like no other. To get her out of my fucking head so I can refocus on my mission. To not let my attraction to Narah or other doubts seep into my thoughts... doubts put there by Ragnar, who keeps trying to imply I should rethink my plan.

"Crius, let me go," Narah gripes, her threat darkening, something I'm particularly fond of.

"I love it when you're angry. Have you ever had hate sex, Narah?"

She scowls as she glares at me over her shoulder, eliciting a burst of laughter out of me.

"I'll take that as a no. When you're ready, I'll show you. You've never experienced anything like it, but I promise you'll scream for more."

"I-I don't know what you're talking about." She glances to where Ragnar walked off.

"Oh, you'll find out," I murmur under my breath.

She looks back at me, and I'm convinced she heard me. Good.

Keeping her against me, it's not hard to see how beautiful she is—fiery amber eyes, full lips I want to bite, and an ass I crave to fuck. I'm fully aware, of the four of us, I'm the only one who hasn't plunged into her cunt, but I've seen the way she studies me, smell her arousal when in my company, and our time is coming. I'll make sure of that, a fleeting thought that passes my mind each time I see her. Lately, my wolf has been growing louder in my head about claiming her.

When she finally calms down, I release her, and she stumbles from my arms before coiling around toward me. The ache on her face touches me. Seeing Ragnar with

Lyssa kills her, and even though Ragnar hates the girl, it doesn't change Narah's hurt.

"It's going to be okay," I suggest, moving toward her. "I promise."

"I just hate all the bullshit politics being played here," she mutters. "There's no way I'm okay with Ragnar having a meal with her... She's not his fucking mate." Her eyes widen.

I adore how passionate she is. Hell, it's giving me goosebumps. I want her to get this fired up over me one day.

"Sometimes, we have to do crap we loathe for the greater good."

She sneers at me, looking ready to sucker punch me in the face for daring to say that. Who is this lioness who has been coming out of her shell? Damn, I love this side of her. She might have appeared meek at the beginning of our mission, but I'm starting to see she had us fooled.

"There's a feast tonight," I explain, taking her back into my arms, though her hands snap up and press against my chest. "We're all invited, so what is the harm of Ragnar sharing one meal with her in our company? The pros are we keep relations strong with her father and have a safe place for your sister while we prepare to go into the Poisonous Woods." The moment the words left my mouth, I realized I'd said the wrong damn thing. Fuck.

"Tomorrow?" she says, her eyes brightening.

"More like the day after," I lie. Ragnar will have my balls for telling Narah our plans. He didn't want her on the mission. *Nice job, Crius.*

"Ragnar needs the Bane Wolves to build his reach and strength to take over Savage Sector," I say softly, leaning my face to hers. "It's gorgeous that you're jealous, but tonight, you'll need to rein it in."

"I'm not sure I can do that." She glowers at me, and I love her all moody and mad.

Without warning, I kiss her, crashing my lips against her, and catch her off guard. She tenses against me, but she's not shoving me away. I leave a trail of kisses across her cheek, then bury my face in the curve of her neck. Inhaling deeply, I drown myself in her spicy, sexy scent. Lips on her warm neck, I kiss and bite, torturing her skin.

"Crius," she mumbles. "We shouldn't be..." Her words turn to moans... and there it is. She fucking wants me just as much as I crave her.

Her shivers against me have my hands falling to her waist, fingers digging into her sides. Just as quickly as I started, I pull back and lick her taste from my lips. She has that stunned expression that turns me on more than she'll ever know. I'm the wolf, and she's my lamb. I love this game.

"Why'd you kiss me?"

"Isn't it obvious?" Sliding my hand down her arm, I pull her hand and press it against my groin over my jeans. My hard cock twitches under her touch, and she doesn't flinch. She holds onto me for a long moment, not backing away, and for the first time, I feel fucking vulnerable and needy. Shit, what the hell is wrong with me?

She lightly squeezes my erection, and I hiss. It feels so good. Then she draws her hand away, smirking, well aware of what she's done. I moan, needing it back, and my wolf coils in my chest, shoving against my insides.

How easy would it be to shove her against the wall, rip off her clothes, and fuck her brains out? The earlier anger vanishes from behind her eyes, and a new look replaces it —desire. She might not say it, but I know she wouldn't push me away if I claimed her now. It's tempting.

"Tonight, we can give Ragnar a show," I suggest, toying with the idea of what I'll do to Narah to drive her insane with arousal. "Make him see what he's missing out on, and if he stops being a dick, he can join us." My words come out without thinking, well aware Ragnar will lose his shit, but when have I ever been to a party that doesn't end in death or sex?

"I'm already one step ahead," she says. "Ragnar already said he'd find a way to accept sharing."

Wait!

"He actually said that?"

"Yep." She gives me a tight nod and slips from my arms. "So, there's no need for your grand plan. I don't even know if I'll go tonight." She makes a hasty retreat toward the mess hall.

Well, color me fucking surprised with Ragnar. Old dogs can learn new tricks after all.

10

NARAH

Crius waves at me from across the grand hall to join him and the other two guys.

They're seated at the farthest possible table, tucked away in the shadows. Rows of long tables with benches are arranged in the room, all pointing to the front where there's a U-shaped table, headed up by the Bane Wolves Pack's Alpha. My gaze finds Ragnar instantly on the Alpha's right-hand side, then Lyssa.

I might be foaming at the mouth with jealousy, seeing her all dolled up in a sapphire green and gold Renaissance gown with a low-cut bust line, her blonde hair falling over her shoulders in soft waves.

I'm wearing a dress Jae borrowed from her friend's mother. I'm not exactly traveling with a bag of clothes, and I've never owned a gown. Looking down, my dress is simple, in a deep burgundy color that cinches at my waist, with long sleeves that ruffle at the wrists and a straight bust line. I pulled my hair back into a ponytail with a few loose strands framing my face. I thought I looked attractive, but next to Lyssa, I might as well be wearing a hessian sack. A deep ache settles in my gut at how awkward I feel.

Ragnar keeps pulling at the high-collared black shirt he wears, looking out of place and uncomfortable. Deep brown hair sits over his shoulder tidily as though he put effort into looking his best.

When he catches my eye from across the room, his lips curl into a smile, and his sky-blue eyes light up. Of course, that's when bitch face notices and reaches over to paw his bicep, releasing a fake laugh.

If I rolled my eyes any harder, I'd lose them somewhere in my head, so instead, I march through the filled room to the back corner. Crius said not to make a scene, and this was for the greater good.

Yeah, well, *my* greater good is all for my sisters. For them, I'll do anything.

Every other seat is taken in the hall, and guards in black uniforms pepper the room, watching. The air thickens with wolf scents, and my wolf stirs, whining at being surrounded by so many Alpha and Beta men who leer at me as I pass them. Their desperate smells invade my nostrils.

Candelabras hang from the arched ceiling, a display of fanned-out swords graces one of the walls, while tapestries of wolves in battle fill the other walls.

My three men smile as their gazes moving up and down my body. I won't deny their attention helps my self-confidence.

"Why are we sitting all the way back here?" I slide in next to Crius while Stone and Nikos sit across from us.

"We had a bet," Nikos says. "And this spot won."

"Do I even want to know what you bet on?" I reach for a breadstick from the wicker basket in the middle of the table and bite into it.

"You," Crius adds, his hand sliding across my lower back. "It was unanimous that you wouldn't want to be close to Lyssa without wanting to gauge her eyes out. Plus, with us having our own party at our table, we didn't want to torture Ragnar any more than he already was."

"Wow, you make me sound so jealous," I mutter, a soft warmth spreading over my cheeks at being so obvious.

"My hummingbird," Crius says, his hand sliding across my back, which felt amazing. "If I hadn't been there to stop you today, you and Lyssa would have gotten into a huge catfight. While I would have loved to watch you kick her butt, this isn't about what you or I want."

"You surprise me, Crius," Nikos responds with a sarcastic smirk. "Since when do you give a fuck about not causing chaos?"

He shrugs and reaches over for a breadstick too. "Ragnar needs this to work. We're not exactly swimming in options."

We all turn and look at Ragnar. Lyssa is leaning against him and staring up at him like a puppy dog while he's in deep conversation with her father.

"He's fuming," Stone states. "Look at how much he's sweating."

"I bet she's feeling him up under the table," Crius adds, and I glare at him for putting that image into my mind.

Nikos howls with laughter. "About time he took one for the team. Most of the time, it's one of us doing something ridiculous."

My glass empty, I spot a jug of wine on the opposite edge of our table beside Crius. The image of me accidentally spilling it onto Lyssa's lap makes me giddy.

"My mouth feels like it's drier than a desert. Can I have some wine, please?"

"Allow me." Crius pours wine into my glass and hands it to me. "Here you go."

"Thanks," I mutter and return to glaring at Lyssa.

Crius turns his attention back to Nikos. "Like the time you got dressed up as an old hag to get us into a pack. Man, I almost pissed my pants when that guard tried to feel you up."

"Wait, what happened?" I ask, caught up in their conversation while the three of them howl with laughter and chug back wine from their metal jugs.

Surprisingly, I find myself partially enjoying the night, listening as they tell stories from their battles in Denmark, even though I keep glancing across the room at Ragnar. I play with the idea of leaving the dinner party and making a quick escape. Just seeing her draped over Ragnar hurts.

As plates of sliced meat and roast vegetables arrive at our table, I ask the guys, "What's the occasion for tonight's gathering, anyway? I mean, the hall is packed, but not everyone from the pack is here." Including all the kids, elderly, and mothers. Men fill the room, outnumbering all other groups, and I won't deny it's slightly unsettling.

"A celebration of Ragnar's return," Stone explains sarcastically. "He and Mihai are making plans tonight on how they'll conquer the Savage Sector."

Mihai... must be the Alpha's name. I just hope whatever they discuss involves rescuing Kaira since I haven't had a chance to catch Ragnar all day to talk.

I swallow a mouthful of what tastes like venison and follow it up with crispy potatoes soaked in dripping butter, which melt on my tongue. It's been too long since I enjoyed a hot roast meal, so I dig in and enjoy every last crumb, including the dessert of bread pudding, all while the guys drink and exchange embarrassing stories about one another.

A loud clapping from the front of the room catches my attention.

Mihai stands from his chair, and the chatter in the room dies down. He's an older man with trimmed white hair and deeply tanned skin. He's wearing dark pants, a fitted white shirt buttoned to his throat, and a jacket hangs on the back of his seat. Despite looking older, muscles fill his shirt.

"Tonight is an auspicious occasion," he begins. "A new beginning for the Bane Wolves. Living in the Savage Sector has always come with its challenges, and for our survival, we need to fight to hold our footing in this world. Daily, other packs encroach closer onto our lands while more undead migrate north. We need to take action before it's too late." His jaw clenches as he talks, but in his eyes, I can see he truly cares for his pack. Everyone hangs off every word, their eyes glued to their

Alpha. Mihai half-turns toward Ragnar and slaps a hand on his shoulder.

"We have joined forces with Ragnar, our northern friend, and his pack. His immense help with the witches and rogue wolf packs will be invaluable, and just as important is that he will join my family once he officially mates with my daughter, Lyssa. They will be the new generation to guide us into leadership and survival."

An explosion of cheering and clapping ensues in the room.

While I'm glaring at them, Lyssa throws her arms around Ragnar. Fire flares through me, my muscles tensing at the sight. *Mating.* What the fuck does that mean? One meal he'd promised her.

Crius' hand slides from my back to my thigh as he leans in close to me. "Mihai's words are empty. We're just biding our time to get the upper hand."

"If you say so," I mumble back, feeling ice cold.

The other men's eyes are still on Mihai, while my heart thumps so hard, it might burst out of my chest and fly away on wings.

"I promise," Crius whispers. His breath across my cheek and his hand sliding under my dress through the high slit on the side warms me.

"Crius." I push against his arm, and he gives me a heated glance.

A young male server, who must be a Beta to be working as a server, arrives at our table to clean up. Alphas wouldn't be caught dead working such menial jobs. They're given to Betas, while we Omegas are used for one thing—rutting and breeding. That's how our cruel world is divided. Three types of wolves, all abiding by a hierarchy and accepting their roles, even if many don't agree with the unfairness. It's utter crap that an Omega is seen as nothing other than making babies by Alphas, while Betas are the inferior wolf and often treated as slaves to Alphas. The only people it doesn't suck for are the Alphas who fight tooth and nail to hold status. The rest of us do our best to just survive.

"Are you finished, miss?" the Beta asks, pointing his chin at my plate and distracting me from my thoughts.

"Yes, thank you." I reach up to give him the plate. Of course, that's the exact moment Crius' hand slides between my legs, brushing against the thin fabric of my underwear.

I gasp loud enough to have the Beta glance my way. My cheeks flush with heat, and his touch awakens my wolf. On cue, she's groaning in my chest for Martell. I fucking hate him, but she holds a candle for him, not knowing any better.

Crius' fingers remain locked under my skirt while he grins at the poor Beta, who looks so confused. Crius leans in, his mouth on my ear.

"Open your sweet legs for me. Let me show you how you'll forget Ragnar right now."

"Have you lost your mind?" My body shakes as I stare at him incredulously. "We're in a room with wolves." I push against his hand, but he's like steel and unmovable.

"Don't make me ask you again. I'm not above dragging you out of here over my shoulder, making it clear to everyone that I'm taking you outside to fuck you. Then I promise you, we'll have an audience."

"You wouldn't," I hiss.

"Don't test me. You've been on my mind all day, thinking about how you groped my cock and our kiss. No one will see us. With so many damn wolf smells in here, we'll be fine."

"*You* forced me to touch you," I snap.

An evil grin splits his mouth, revealing a line of white teeth. He wriggles his fingers across the apex of my thighs, and every small caress sends a jolt of arousal through my body. It doesn't take long for liquid heat to soak my underwear. I hate myself for being so weak when these men push me to my limits.

He presses so close against me, I couldn't slide a piece of paper between us if I tried, while my breath wedges in my lungs along with my whining wolf.

I'm staring into his eyes, and he's grinning.

"Shall we?" he asks.

"You're an ass," I growl. Tingles race down my spine that I'm even contemplating it, knowing he'll carry out his threat.

"And you're aching for me," he whispers. "Now, open up and look at me. I want to see the moment you melt and come undone all over my fingers."

Frantically, I look around. Stone and Nikos are oblivious, their backs to us as they stare at Mihai, who's still talking.

I must be crazy, widening my legs slightly, thankful my dress is long. I give him my best death glare when he pushes the scrap of material of my panties aside. Shivering against him, our eyes lock as his fingers slide across the slick seam of my pussy. Barely able to catch my breath, I'm startled. His hand is on me... in my panties... at the pack gathering. I bite my lip, refusing to make a sound, but my widening eyes give me away. The reaction on Crius' face is lustful.

He glides his finger between my folds, and a flaring need consumes me. My nipples tighten to hard points and push into the fabric of my dress. I give him my best death glare, or at least attempt to, but when his finger applies pressure to my clit and rubs me, I moan. Gripping the edge of the table, suddenly, I don't care that there are dozens of people in this room who could glance our way and see his hand under my skirt.

"You're a very brave girl, Narah," he whispers in my ear.

Am I brave or just someone who is constantly horny for these men and can't seem to say no to them?

He adjusts himself next to me. "Scooch forward a bit," he asks. Crazily, I listen to him and do just that.

There's no warning before he pushes two fingers into me. Arching in my seat, I pull my lower lip between my teeth, biting down to stop myself from moaning. It feels incredible, and every inch of me is bursting to scream and let my body ride the wave he's forced through me.

"You haven't told me to stop, Narah," he teases. "Why's that?"

I blink at him, my brain foggy, my body buzzing.

"Because you threatened me?"

"It's not like you to give in that easily. You know what I think? You've wanted me from the beginning."

His fingers work their way in and out of me, his thumb on my clit, making me lose my mind. What were we talking about again?

"That..." I trail off as he fingers me faster. "Crius," I breathe his name so softly, I have no idea if I made a sound.

"Is this how you like to be touched?"

He's fucking with my brain.

A shadow falls over us, and I stiffen, glancing up, half blushing, half about to scream with an orgasm.

It's the Beta guy again, placing several plates of fruit, nuts, and cheeses on our table.

"Eyes on me," Crius whispers in my ear, and I lift my attention to him, holding his gaze. "I've waited a long time for this." His fingers move in a different way, and my hips rock, and my breaths are heavier.

Clutching his arm, my nails dig into his flesh, but his fingers never pause. The way he stares at me with his evil grin dares me to lose control. I see it in his hungry eyes, his greedy fingers driving me over the edge.

My skin tightens, and my body is on fire.

One whimper from me, and his fingering destroys me. My mind explodes, and my body shakes. I arch my back, keeping my mouth shut, which is close to impossible as a climax rocks through me. Pleasure digs deep within me, completely ruining me as I come on Crius' hand. My walls squeeze him, and every movement he makes, his thumb never ceasing to tease my clit, heightens the sensation.

He holds me close as I twitch uncontrollably, and I bury my face in his neck, the cry strangling me coming out against the heat of his skin.

"You are beautiful," he whispers. "So much more than I ever expected when you climax."

When I finally settle down, my head spins from how intensely I came. I've never felt it burst through me like that. Crius withdraws his fingers, and my body sways as I lift my head from his neck and realize we have an audience after all. The Beta's face is red, his mouth gaping open. It's clear he knows exactly what had just happened to me.

"You've had your show, now fuck off," Crius growls, sending the server scurrying out of the hall.

When I twist around, Stone and Nikos are leering at me with primal hunger in their eyes, and in the distance, Ragnar's looking our way.

Did he see everything?

Crius brings his fingers to his mouth and licks them clean, smirking. "Delicious."

"Whatever the hell I just witnessed, I want in," Nikos states, while Stone nods frantically.

I'm still coming down from my high, and the earlier need consumes me. Despite being watched and knowing they'll never let me forget this, there is no way I can deny that was fucking amazing.

11

RAGNAR

"**R**agnar, just one dance," Lyssa drawls, her eyes batting with desperation.

Every time she touches me, my skin crawls.

The girl's touch shouldn't revolt me. She's beautiful, and when I first entered the treaty deal with the Bane Wolves, I considered her a good mate for fucking and breeding. There was no love or longing between us, and that hasn't changed. The decision was made when I first arrived at the Savage Sector from my home in Denmark, and I was eager to establish a foothold in Romania.

Now, I'm a different man, and my sights are set on my little fox, Narah. She sits in the rear of the room with my men, and I would have to be a fool not to see Crius enjoying himself with her, pushing her. My muscles tense, and my hands stiffen by my side. The guy knows exactly how to press a girl's buttons, and it takes every inch of strength not to storm over and rip him from her side.

Except I've made her a promise, haven't I? Fuck.

My men are like my brothers, and Narah has become my fascination. Who am I kidding? I'm fucking obsessed with her, lost to her, and there's nothing I wouldn't do to keep her by my side, even go against my instincts.

"Ragnar, are you listening?" Lyssa pesters me.

I shake my thoughts away, then glance at her.

"A meal was all I offered you," I shoot back and climb to my feet. I've had enough of being a damn monkey on show for everyone. All this time wasted. Mihai and I could have been working on plans to take over Savage Sector, determining which packs we'd attack first and which we would try to win over without resorting to combat. I'm suffocating between him and Lyssa, both putting on a show to their people.

I question if it wouldn't be a good time to educate them on the undead migrating to this sector and teach them how to fight the new threat instead of placating them.

"Ragnar," Lyssa pleads, reaching for my hand, but I leave her behind, needing fresh air.

Before I even make it to the door, Mihai is by my side. He sets a large hand on my shoulder, pausing me in my escape.

"The people are scared," he says in a hush. "Let them see some merriment in their lives, some hope. I have arranged for a band, so everyone can dance, with you and Lyssa taking the lead. Watching you enjoying yourself, they'll be less afraid."

I grind my back teeth. "Maybe they should be terrified."

I take a step forward, and the hand on my shoulder tightens.

"I'm not asking, Ragnar. This is something my pack needs. After this, we'll make plans and maybe discuss once more the number of females you'll bring me. Forty is low... maybe I can sweeten your deal for more females."

My body tenses and I want to squeeze the life out of Mihai for pressing me to dance with Lyssa, for wanting to negotiate our agreement. I have yet to travel to Shadowlands Sector and convince Dušan, the Alpha there, to sell me forty Omegas, and I'm not prepared to budge on that number.

I lift my gaze to Narah, who's laughing with my men, and a different kind of rage unleashes. The wolf inside me rages that we're not with her instead of playing politics. He's been drawn to her since the first time we met at a bar, where she approached me for my help with her sisters. At first, I put it down to her being just another beautiful face, even if my wolf was crazed around her. In hindsight, I see it was easier to ignore the obsession she's become.

"One dance to get everyone else in the spirit," Mihai buzzes in my ear. "Then you and I will head to my office. Bring Nikos, too. It'll be good to have another strategic viewpoint."

Keeping my eyes on Narah, I remind myself as much as I want to say fuck it all, I can't forget the bigger picture. There won't be a welcome party if I return to Denmark, not after I left the country in what my father would consider a disgrace by simply walking away from him.

Let's be honest; he had no plans to hand his pack over to me. The bastard would live forever to ensure he never lost power. Remaining under his reign would end with me murdering him, so I left.

I have every intention of showing that prick I don't need him. That I can build a future for myself in the Savage Sector. Then I can rescue my sister, Hel, who Father sold her to our enemies to marry their warlord. Clenching my teeth, I look back at Narah. She always makes me forget how savage this world can be.

Sacrifices—we all make them, even if this shit infuriates me.

I turn back toward Mihai, who smiles and pats my shoulder. The urge to break his arm in several places might bring me joy, but I opt to play his game. I grew up in a pack where no one could be trusted, and if you didn't manipulate others, you were as good as dead, so this is nothing new to me.

"Fine," I murmur.

"Good man," he says as I lift my gaze to Lyssa, who's already rushing toward me eagerly. I take a deep breath and remind myself... it's just one fucking dance.

CRIUS

"**A**re you kidding me?" Narah murmurs under her breath, her eyes glued on Ragnar and Lyssa on the dance floor.

They look so damn awkward, I almost burst out laughing at how she's practically strangling him. She's wrapped around him, her cheek attached to his chest, while he's only holding onto her shoulders.

One way or another, he'll have to deal with Lyssa and her father.

I'll admit the dance surprises me. Ragnar does everything with purpose, so I trust there's a good reason behind it. Especially when he was cursing her like a storm before we arrived at the hall.

Nikos had left to join Mihai, who summoned him for a strategic talk after the dance, and Stone was strolling across the room to track down a server for more wine.

I turn back to Narah, only to watch the precious little thing running across the room and bursting out of the hall. She's so mad at Ragnar, it makes me grin. Her emotions are explosive.

Hell, this was going to blow up.

I jolt to my feet and take fast steps right behind her. Someone has to defuse the situation, so it looks like I'm the man for the job. Drawing in the fresh air, the cool breeze washes over me. There's movement to my left, and I catch the flash of her burgundy dress disappearing behind a hut and take off after her.

Catching up to her, I think about how I'd love to chase her down in a real cat-and-mouse game and make her all mine once I capture her. Even now, the way her sweet ass moves with her fast steps consumes me. Her scent from fingering her remains in my nostrils, the smell as delicious as she tastes.

A small tease that's nowhere near enough... not even close.

She rushes down a dirt path, which will eventually bring her to the town's lake.

"You can stop now." I grab her arm as I reach her. When she swings around to me, she's scowling, and her eyes glisten with tears.

My heart shudders at her pain.

"Lyssa means nothing to Ragnar. I'll stake my life on it," I say, feeling compelled to convince her. Taking her hand, she rips it away. There's more than jealousy on her face.

"I'm so furious with myself," she finally admits. "I've become so damn weak. The way I reacted back there is stupid, but if I went back inside and saw them, I'd be no different. My plan was to rescue my sisters, then I went and got feelings for Ragnar, for all of you damn Alphas. Now, look at me. I'm shaking with anger because I'm jealous." She lowers her gaze as though her words strike a chord.

She is absolutely stunning, even more so because she's angry for liking us.

"Wow, that's actually the nicest thing you've said to me," I say sarcastically.

She doesn't bite back, marching to where the town's lights fade behind us.

"Why are you out here, putting yourself in danger if you're so worried about protecting your sisters?"

"I'm furious at myself and at how easily I let emotions control me. That's how you get killed in this world."

"So does walking in the woods alone at night."

She cuts me a glance. "I've got you with me, don't I?"

"I can only do so much against a horde of zombies." The thought has me glancing around, aware we're still within the confines of the Bane Wolves' territory, fencing all around. I've also seen first-hand accounts of how relentless these fuckers are when it comes to reaching their next meal.

"See over there." She points ahead of us through a small clearing between several fern trees. "There's a lofty wire fence, and it looks untouched to me. I think we'll be safe."

I squint through the dark, and the metal fence catches the moonlight. "You've been here before?"

"Ended up joining my sister on a fishing expedition with a few families."

Silence beats between us.

"Caring for us doesn't make you weak, Narah. It makes you a fighter."

"My father once told me people who have nothing left to lose are the most dangerous. I don't consider myself a fighter or strong, more of a survivor."

"What do you think a survivor is? The strongest people because nothing stops them." Her words bring her father to mind and how he's now undead. I am remorseful about keeping secrets from Narah, but Ragnar made us promise not to upset her with what her mother has done. I've always been a man to speak honestly and say it as it is. While I understand why Ragnar made the call he did, I would have already told Narah the truth if it was my call.

"How about we head back to our hut?" I suggest as worry flows over her expression once more. "There are several pillows in there you can punch and pretend they're Lyssa's head."

"That actually sounds like fun." The moonlight reflects in Narah's amber eyes.

"Done." I stick out my hand, which she gingerly accepts, then we walk to the small home on the edge of the village we've been given for our stay.

Though, to be honest, my suggestion is completely selfish. Ever since I enjoyed her pussy, my cock hasn't gone down, and I intend to have her all to myself for a few hours.

"By the way, that dominating thing you did at the party was a dick move," she says, not looking at me.

"I didn't see you complaining, and that was just the beginning."

Her huffs break into a laugh.

Challenge accepted.

Not that I need much motivation. Her scent remains lodged in my head, teasing me with what I need to achieve my peak. When she had no real resistance at the party gathering, I knew then she'd have me worshiping her. I'm ready to make her wildest dreams come true as long as it involves me.

"It's still a dick move," she grumbles and pouts.

Something savage, primal, comes over me, an intensifying need that is all-consuming. This walk is taking way too fucking long. I pivot around to step in her path, my hands falling to her hips, and lift her off her feet, then walk her back so fast, she has no time to complain. Pressing her against the closest tree, I can't help but smile at her shocked gasp.

Her hands snap up, flat on my chest, but a little too late. She's already mine.

"You like me? Fucking fantastic, Narah. Now, how about we do something about that?"

"Put me down," she growls, pushing against my chest.

"There's my Narah. I want you angry and take out your fury on me. I'm going to fuck that tight pussy until you forget your own name." Pressing my body to hers, I hear her heartbeat thumping faster. Such a beautiful sound.

Not wasting a second, I drive my hand up her dress. With a single snap of my fingers, I rip off her underwear and shove the scraps of fabric into the pocket of my pants.

"Crius... shit!"

"Game's changed, my hummingbird. I'm in charge now."

She swallows hard, staring at me, not quite believing I have her caged and bare.

"What do you want to do, fuck me? Your cock is hard, and your balls are hurting after your stunt at the party," she bites out. "Maybe you deserve to hurt."

"Good, keep going," I snarl as my wolf thrusts forward, urging me not to stop. I want her to use me as her punching bag. This is what she's been demanding with her actions. "Get it all out of your system, and when you calm down, I'll show you what a goddess you are." I don't waste a second and press my knee between her legs, spreading them for me.

"Tell me, is this what you want?" I shove her dress aside and unbuckle my pants with one hand. My cock jolts to attention upon release, and I hiss at how good it feels to unleash him. Pressing the tip to her drenched cunt, I met her gaze. She's slightly panicked and looks around at the houses in the distance. There's no one around, and even if they were, I'd tell them to piss off. I'm not letting go of my delicious treat.

Still, she doesn't tell me to stop. Panting, her hands grip my shirt as her pupils dilate with lust.

"You smell fucking incredible," I growl against her neck as the tip of my cock teases her entrance, and it's killing me. I crave to feel her wrapped around me, sucking me down.

"I wanted my first time with you to be gentle, but I can't wait much longer, Narah. Ready?" I groan.

"Fuck you, Crius, for making me want this so badly."

Laughter bursts from my throat, and she stares at me with lust in her eyes. Oh, she has no idea what I have in store for her.

"I'll do my best to not tear you in two."

Her eyes widen, but I'm already pressing into her while guiding her legs to wrap around my waist. Once I have her in position, placing a hand on her back so the tree won't scratch her back, I sink into her, tight walls squeezing around me. I want her stretched. Her nails dig into my shoulders as I move in and out, quickening my thrusts.

"I want every inch of you," I say, breathing heavily

"You can have me," she moans as her head falls to my shoulder. Her eyes flutter, and she shivers in my arms as her pussy tightens around my cock.

Fuck me, she's everything I crave.

Pulling her away from the tree, I cup her ass with two hands as I bounce her up and down on my dick. Her lips are on my neck, and she bites down into the tender curve, her chest arching against me. I howl as her sharp teeth sink into flesh, driving me to madness. Pain and pleasure are my thing. My cock twitches as the heightened climax claws through me, but it's too fast. I'm not even close to finishing with Narah.

Sliding out of her, I lower her to her feet, and her dress tumbles down to cover her gorgeous offering. Tucking my cock back in, it hurts to trap him back in my pants.

She gives me a wonky look. "What are you doing?"

"I don't want to knot in you just yet. I intend on fucking you a lot more before we go down that path." Not waiting for her response, I take her hand and rush us across the village at ultra-speed, and we're in the hut before I can say, *let's get to fucking.*

Kicking the door shut, I reach for her dress, and my wolf's claws extend just long enough to rip the dress off her body. She gasps as shreds of red fabric cascade, unveiling a body I'm about to worship.

"Shit, that's not my dress," she groans.

"I don't give a fuck. Now, come over here." I seize her arm and spin her around to face away from me, then bend her over the arm of the couch.

She cries out at how fast I move her, which only makes me grin. Impatient and my erection straining, I rapidly strip from my clothes and kick them aside, then turn to my girl, who's starting to get up.

"Don't move." Running my hand up her spine, I force her back down. "I want your ass high and your legs spread. Tell me how much you want this, Narah… beg me for it."

When she doesn't respond but narrows her gaze at me over her shoulder, I slap her adorable ass, then grab and grope it.

"Ouch," she cries, and I love the sound she makes.

"You are so beautiful, Narah, but that's not going to mean I'll let you off easily."

"You know what I want," she purrs, her grin devious.

"Say it." I squeeze her ass cheek as my thumb brushes small circles of her rear entry.

Her body shivers, and her hips rock, pressing against my hand for more. She's drenched, making my thumb slippery. I slip the tip of my thumb into her ass, just enough to tempt her, and her moans bring me off-the-chart pleasure. I palm my cock with my other hand and push a bit more into her gorgeous little ass.

"Crius," she begs.

"Ah, there it is. Let me hear it."

"Fuck... fuck me like an animal. Make me scream."

"Oh, my hummingbird, that's it," I growl and reward her by fingering her ass.

Her scream is mesmerizing.

My dick throbs at the sight of my thumb going in and out of her rear, of her swollen, wet pussy on display as her legs spread wider. She's ready... so damn ready, I can't wait another second.

I slip between her legs, drawing my thumb out of that gorgeous hole. Gripping my cock, I guide it to where it belongs, sinking back into her cunt. She grips me tightly as her glistening lips swallow my cock.

"Narah," I gasp when she squeezes her walls around me. Adjusting slightly, I hammer into her, slow to get a feel for her. When it comes to doggy style, I can reach much deeper inside her.

"That's it. Fuck me hard."

Gripping her hip, my other hand curls around her hair and pulls her head back just enough, it's the kind of pain that gets her off. I rock into her, forgetting where one of us starts and the other ends. I never would have guessed my little bird likes to be pounded this way. The sounds of slapping echo around us, but her cries are louder.

"Oh My Fucking God!" she screams, which only pushes me faster to the point that with each thrust, the couch moves across the floor.

Hearing a gasp to my left, I twist my head to see Stone walking into the hut, his mouth gaping open and lust already bulging in his pants.

"What the fuck?!" he blurts, breaking my perfect rhythm.

Narah tenses beneath me, then turns her head toward Stone as he shuts the door behind him.

"You bastards left me all alone in that boring-as-shit party to have sex? That's just cruel." He's already ripping off his clothes. "For that, I'm joining in."

"That isn't why I left," she gasps, breathing heavily. "But yes, come over here, big boy."

Stone practically rips his pants off, then struts toward us, his cock hard. Narah gawks at him while I'm still deep inside her.

"I'm not a crossing-swords kinda guy, so if you can deal with that, join us." I have no issues sharing with the three other guys, as long as the focus is Narah.

Stone moves to stand next to Narah and cups her face. "You're such a good girl, aren't you? And you're going to be rewarded now. Come climb me like a tree." Stone glances at me. "You good to take her from the rear?"

"I want this," Narah purrs, looking at me with pleading eyes. How can I resist that look?

"Sure, just waltz in here and take over," I growl at Stone. "You're just lucky I'm so fucking horny right now, I'll do anything to push my cock back into our beauty."

"You owe me this for ditching me at the party."

"Damn, what are you, five years old?" I gripe, slipping out of Narah. Slipping an arm under her stomach, I lift her to her feet.

"When it comes to sex with my sweetheart, I don't give a fuck what you call me." Stone tenderly pulls Narah to stand in front of him, both of them naked, face to face, and they kiss.

Sure, I'm fucking mad he's acting like a dick, but Narah's enjoying herself, and ultimately that's what I want, right? Besides, this is just the beginning. Now that she's opened the flood gates, so to speak, about our sex life, she has no clue what's coming her way.

The way she scorches me with her body has me prowling toward her. Narah draws me to stand behind her, sandwiched between Stone and me, in the middle of the room.

"I want you both at the same time."

"That's my girl." Stone lifts her off her feet, and she wraps her legs around his hips.

With a smirk, I step closer to my girl, pressing my chest flush to her back, with my cock cradled against her full ass. I embrace her and take her full breasts with both hands, kneading them, my fingers lavishing her nipples, pinching. She likes a bit of pain with her arousal.

She turns her head toward me, her eyes full of desire, and I claim her mouth, tasting her sweetness. Pressing my tongue to the seam of her lips, I demand her surrender. I crave to dominate her, to let every inch of me consume her.

She stiffens, moaning, and I realize the greedy bastard who interrupted us is pushing his cock into her. My competitive nature plunges through me, and I seize my cock, positioning myself at her ass.

"You ready?" I whisper against her mouth.

"Please," she moans. Pinned between us, she makes small impatient sounds.

I run my tip over her drenched ass before gently pressing into her, then find the perfect rhythm with Stone. She's so wet and ready to go.

She clenches her muscles at first, squeezing me. Stone hisses, feeling the same sensation.

"We'll take it slow at first. Now, let us in," I say.

"Do you like this?" Stone mutters.

"I'm ready to explode and can't get enough. Of course, I blame Crius for bringing this wild side out in me."

I laugh. "The blame is mine, and I'll own it."

"I adore the full of lust look in your eyes," Stone adds. "You are perfect like this, dripping over my cock. You are doing so well."

Bracing herself, we all shift slightly as we find our standing position. With my powerful arms, I hold on to her ass while Stone grasps her hips, and we slowly push back into her until we find the right positioning between us. Locked in a lover's embrace, Narah pinned between us, we thrust harder, falling into a pattern that has Narah crying out for more. She's absolutely stunning during sex.

"Where the hell is Ragnar now?" Stone mutters between thrusting and Narah's sweet cries. "He needs to see how perfect we are when we share."

"He'll find out soon enough." I try to catch my breath as we thrust faster, and the build-up tears through me.

Narah's body shudders, her back glistening with sweat, while Stone's chest heaves for air. Then she convulses in our arms, screaming as an orgasm claims her.

When she squeezes my cock, I roar with how much it hurts, how incredible it feels.

Stone snarls and his eyes flutter back.

"Don't you fucking lose control," I bark. "She needs to climax at least three more times before we flood her with our seed. Don't you fucking knot," I growl.

"Three, are you crazy?" she murmurs.

"Chill, buddy," Stone rasps. "I have control."

Holding on to my girl, wrapping her in my arms, I pull out of her and draw her off Stone's cock. Her legs wobble, so I lift her into my arms. Stone follows us to the bed, never taking his eyes off Narah, who's still high from her amazing climax.

I lay her on the bed and push the hair out of her face. Her body is heaven—bouncy tits, curvy hips, and a pussy I'm dying to suck. "You're so sexy." Climbing in next to her, I glide my hand along her jaw as Stone throws himself alongside her on the bed, making the whole damn hut shake.

My cock pulses, and adrenaline thumps in my veins.

"Catch your breath, gorgeous, because I want you to ride my face," I tell her.

"I'd like that." She smiles, looking from me to Stone. "Ragnar was my first, so I never knew being with two men could be so incredible. So, how about this? I ride your face while I suck Stone's cock?"

"Fuck, yes," Stone bellows.

I take her into my arms and pepper her face with kisses.

"Tomorrow, you won't be able to walk straight by the time we're finished with you."

She grins and kisses me quickly on the lips.

"Is that a promise?"

12

NARAH

Sleep clings to my mind. It's too early for anyone to be up, so it's alarming to wake up and find myself alone after falling asleep in Stone and Crius' arms.

And the first thing I feel is my wolf, sitting in my chest heavily, furiously snarling at me for betraying our fated mate.

I grind my jaw, so exhausted from this shit.

The cool air brushes through my hair just outside the hut, and morning frays at the edges of the horizon, painting the sky in oranges and purples. It's spectacular. I might enjoy it more if I knew where all the guys had gone and my wolf would chill the hell out.

Last night, I sensed Nikos joining us. Ragnar had been there too, but he kept to himself, mostly. I'd been too tired to make a big deal of it.

Where would all four of them go before dawn?

I continue down the dirt path toward the mess hall, figuring they might be early risers; at least, that's what I tell myself. Something feels off about the day, and it's barely started. Night still has shadows surrounding the village, though locals are already milling about the village.

"Look what the wolf dragged out of bed," Lyssa gripes as she steps into my path from behind a home.

I sigh heavily. She's the last person I want to face right now as I stifle a yawn. I'm not awake enough to deal with her, especially when she looks immaculate with her hair pinned off her face and cascading down her back. What time did she wake up to look so perfect? I quickly run my fingers through my hair since I haven't had a chance to comb it.

"I asked you a question," she whines, folding her arms across her chest.

"In fact, you didn't. You made a stupid remark that isn't even correct. It's 'look what the cat dragged in.'" I blink at her while she scrunches her nose at me as if I'm wrong. "Listen, I don't know what you want, but I'm not in the mood." Sidestepping her, I groan under my breath.

Apparently, that gives her the opening she needs. She snatches my arm, her nails digging into flesh. I spin toward her, tugging my arm from her grip.

"Don't think I didn't hear you screaming like a slut in your hut last night, being fucked like the whore you are."

I rear my shoulders back, my mind thinking about how crazy Crius and Stone drove me, how they'd brought me to orgasm three times. Had I been so loud, others in the pack heard us? Shit.

With the way she's glaring at me, instead of embarrassment, anger climbs through me.

"It was an incredible night, one you'll never experience." I hate being bitchy, but Lyssa is pushing my buttons when I have zero patience.

"Ha," she bellows. "I know you're jealous of Ragnar and me, so you fucking his men makes you so desperate. He spent the whole party with me."

My response flew out of my mouth before I could stop myself.

"And he spent the night with me."

Her mouth drops open, and she slaps the right side of my face, dragging her claws across my cheek. The pain is sharp and stings like hell.

Instinct kicks in, and I sweep my arm up, knocking hers aside, then kick her knee, leaving a dirty footprint on her white jeans. Better yet, she loses her balance and tumbles into a mud puddle next to the path.

I touch my throbbing cheek and come back with spots of blood on my fingertips.

Goddammit.

I should laugh in her face, but I can't bring myself to do it. She looks pitiful enough as it is, and the fact I know why she's behaving like this makes it harder. Ragnar needs to tell her the truth because things are getting out of hand. And while he's at it, he can tell me what the hell is going on between us.

"You fucking cow," she snaps, pushing herself up off the ground, her white pants covered in mud. She sneers at me, her upper lip curling and a death stare behind her gaze. "I've actually been nice to you. Hell knows why."

I roll my eyes hard. She has no idea what 'nice' means.

"I haven't told you the secret Ragnar's keeping from you since I felt sorry for you, but after that move, you can forget it."

"I don't care what you have to say." I turn to leave, clenching my jaw.

"Ragnar was meant to kill your mother," she announces, and I can hear the smile in her voice at how much pleasure it gives her to tell me this.

I pause, trying to make sense of what she's saying, but a dozen or more questions pop into my mind, and a cold flare rushes down my arms. I turn around to face her once more, my stomach flips with unease as though it knows something bad is about to happen.

"What do you mean?"

I stand several feet from her where she's slouching on one leg, her hands deep in the pockets of her pants.

"Having the Alpha as my father, I hear a lot of things."

"And... what did you hear?"

She smiles, and I really hate this girl.

"Months ago, he told Father about meeting a hunter from Storm Wolves, who offered him a decent payment to hunt down an older female. She ran from her husband and three daughters, and their pack wanted her back at any cost. After you came to town, I started digging around about you. When I found out where you're from, I put two and two together. There aren't many families blessed enough to have three daughters. When I asked Ragnar, he didn't deny it."

My heart races at her words while my mind frantically tries to piece the past together with her reveal. At that stage, I doubt Ragnar knew my mother carried magic. Otherwise, the Alpha of Storm Wolves would have killed my sisters and me long ago. So, yeah, he might have been asked to do it.

"Why are you telling me? I know, for a fact, he didn't complete his mission."

She strolls toward me with a leering expression.

"Whether he actively hunted your mother down and perhaps never found her isn't really the issue now, is it? It's that he never told you about it, did he? So, how can you really trust him? What other secrets has he kept from you? Like, did you know he has plans to secure Savage Sector, then go save his sister, who was married off to another pack?"

I lift my chin, hating what she's implying.

"I don't have time for your stupid games, Lyssa." Turning on my heels, I march out of there, simmering at letting myself listen to her and that Ragnar didn't tell me. My breath catches as her words fill my ears.

"Relationships aren't based on selling your body, Narah. It's about trust and not hiding secrets."

"Fuck off," I growl and put more distance between us. I march out of the village, down the steps toward the entry gate, needing to be as far from her as possible.

If Lyssa put it together, surely Ragnar did, too, so he knew who my mother was when he met her in the Wolf Mountains. Same with his sister. I know it's not crucial to our mission, but I was a fool to think I meant enough to him, that he'd share important things about himself. I shouldn't care, but it weighs on me. Damn Lyssa, I'm letting her gaslight me. So what if Ragnar didn't tell me? They aren't exactly details that would have come up in our conversations, and Lyssa is only causing trouble.

Raised voices catch my attention from the gate farther to my right between the guards and someone on the other side of the closed gates. The man is wearing a wide-brimmed hat that sits lopsided on his head and a thick coat that hits mid-thigh, and it's done up to his throat. It's peculiar since the weather isn't cold enough to be so warmly dressed up.

"Ragnar," he says in slow motion and loudly. "I'm here to see him."

He's alone behind the gate, and I'm curious to see who he is.

One of the guards marches in my direction, not paying attention until he lifts his gaze and sees me.

"Oh, it's you," he says haughtily. "Have you seen Ragnar? Be a good girl and go collect him. He has a visitor," he orders me.

My skin crawls at the degrading way he speaks to me.

"I don't know where he is. I'm searching for him, too."

The guard huffs and curses under his breath before storming past me.

I find myself stepping toward the gate out of pure curiosity, along with Lyssa's words that linger on my mind about me not knowing Ragnar. Light footsteps take me closer when the man looks up in my direction.

Amber eyes—just like mine—look back at me.

My feet pause and seem to glue themselves to the ground while my whole body runs cold.

Daddy?

My pulse thunders in my temples.

Am I seeing things?

He's dead... he has to be dead.

I buried his body near the Storm Wolves compound. I cried for weeks. I sat by his grave, talking to him.

"Goodbye, Daddy," I whispered to the fresh grave, well aware that I would carry this moment with me for eternity. An ache in my heart that will never find closure when I doubt I can ever truly accept he's gone. Taken from us because our mom ran from the pack.

Kaira and Jae are kneeling beside me near his grave, crying softly, while Storm Wolves' members walk past us, not paying their respect. No one does, even though he had once ruled this pack as their Alpha. They go about their normal lives while I mourn how lost I feel in this world. How much I hate everyone, except my two sisters. They are all I have left.

Drawing them toward me, we hug as they whimper, their tears soaking my dress. I can't stop crying. Closing my eyes, the breeze stirs across my teary face as I hold my sisters close, unsure how I'm supposed to face another day without my dad.

I'm suffocating on the inside because this can't be real—it can't be—yet I force my legs to move and rush to the gate.

"Miss, do you know this man?" one of the guards asks.

I grasp the metal gate, staring into familiar eyes.

"Is it really you?" My voice chokes with tears.

"You look so sad, girl," he says, his expression unmoving, though it's hard to see since his hat shades half his face.

"Daddy, is that you?" I ask stubbornly, annoyed he's not reacting to seeing me. Has it been that long? "It's me, Narah." My words hang between us, and my mind races. The only undead are zombies, and he's behaving like one.

He blinks, then stares at me blankly. There's something odd about him; his skin a few shades too pale. Tears keep springing to my eyes the longer I stare at him in disbelief. Reaching out to touch him, to make sure I'm not imagining him, he pulls back from my touch.

"Is this man your father?" the guard asks, but I ignore him.

"Daddy, do you recognize me?"

He shakes his head. "Should I?"

I pull back, stumbling a few steps, my chest feeling as if it's being carved in half. It has to be a mistake. A man who looks identical to my father but is not him. All the broken parts inside me float to the surface—the agony, the loneliness, the heartache.

I'm a wreck, staring at this man who shows no emotion.

A horse's neigh from behind me startles me. I flinch and whip around to see Ragnar walking a large black toward the gate. He's dressed for travel in his leather jacket zipped to his throat and riding boots. Behind him are the other three men, each of them with a horse... one for each. It's clear as day, they had every intention of leaving the pack this morning.

Without me.

The other guard from the gate charges up alongside them. "That's him," he says, pointing to the gate. "He's asking for you." He glances at Ragnar, then walks back to his post.

"Narah, what are you doing here?" Ragnar studies me like I'm the last person he expects to find standing here as if I've caught him doing something he shouldn't.

I'm shaking from the overwhelming sensation that I'm about to discover something I don't want to hear. My breath speeds up, and I stare at Stone, Crius, and Nikos, and that same guilty look appears on their faces.

My heart pounds in my chest, and the thought crosses my mind that I made a terrible mistake letting Ragnar and his men become the center of my life. I try very hard not to think about him betraying me, but it's close to impossible.

Ragnar looks past my shoulder to the man I swear is my father. The man who's now calling out his name and confusing me.

"Just tell me, is that my father?" My voice shakes, and tears spill from my eyes. I'm barely holding it together.

"Yes, but it's complicated."

I don't hear anything else before I'm crying, completely wrecked. My world is spinning, and my chest squeezes with agony I never wanted to feel again—grief, mourning, and deception. With it, a sense of betrayal sinks through me that perhaps Lyssa was right.

I don't really know Ragnar.

13

NARAH

"Please, tell me, what's going on?" I plead with Ragnar in a choked voice as he takes me aside by my elbow, as far from the gate as possible. I look back to where Nikos is talking to my dad, Stone and Crius flanking his sides.

Why doesn't my dad recognize me? What's going on?

All I can think about is that I'd buried the wrong person back in Storm Wolves.

I turn back toward Ragnar, and my anger flares. I've had enough of dragging this out. Tugging my arm from his grip, I dig my heels into the supple soil.

"Enough, Ragnar. What the hell is going on? Why is my dead father here? Why doesn't he recognize me, yet he's asking for you?" Shaking and hugging myself, everything in my world feels broken beyond repair. "How long have you known that my dad is alive?"

Ragnar sighs, and there's darkness in his expression as though it pains him to respond.

"Just tell me, please. I can't live another moment not knowing."

"Oh, Narah. This is hard for me to say, but you need to know the truth." He reaches a hand out to me, but I brush him away, my shoulders rising as I'm torn in so many directions.

"Just fucking tell me already. And while you're at it, you can tell me why you thought it was your decision to keep such a secret from me. He's my father. Shouldn't I have known?" Ranting, my anger and frustration pour out of me. If my heart wasn't already broken from Dad's death and more recently, losing my mother, it is now. Seeing my father guts me into tiny pieces. I'm barely holding it together, and the tears refuse to stop falling.

Ragnar's brow furrows, his lips pinching. "I tried to protect you, Narah, but you're right. I should have been upfront."

"Yes, you should have." Despite looking into his eyes and seeing the pain behind them, I'm too angry to care about anything but the truth. No matter what it is, I can take it.

"Okay, Narah." He sounds downhearted. "After your kidnapping, we discovered what your mother has been doing to gain her power."

I blink at him, realizing I hadn't shared with Ragnar what my mother told me about who we were—sorceresses. Ice fills my veins before he even speaks, suspecting what he'll say.

"She's been killing the local villagers in the Wolf Mountains, draining them of energy to feed her magic. Power she used to revert your father from his undead state to what you see out there." His chin points to the gates.

I mull over his words, but I'm numb. I didn't expect the part about my father.

"Sh-She brought him back?" Turning toward my father, he's talking to Stone, his arms almost animated. "She fed him magic, so maybe his memory will come back as he keeps healing, right? Then he'll remember me," I murmur under my breath, my chest squeezing so tight with the hope I'll have Dad back.

"Narah." Taking my hand, Ragnar forces me to face him and stares at me with pain. "She killed dozens of people. We found their bodies piled high in her basement. And your father is not back to normal. Unless he's fed a constant supply of energy drawn from other people, he'll revert to his zombie state. I don't know how many days he has left like this."

Silence hangs between us, and my head is spinning. Mom killed all those people to bring back my dad. "Why? She missed him?" I whisper to myself, barely able to manage words. I'm shaking, trying to process everything. *If she was lonely, why did she leave Jae, Kaira, and me at the mercy of the Storm Wolves?*

"I think she took him from his grave years ago and kept him in his undead form in the basement of her home. I found worn chains bolted to the walls under her house. Then she killed enough people in the village without drawing attention to herself. She fed her empowered blood to him, but he's missing a lot of memories, Narah. He doesn't recall you and your sisters."

He takes my arm; a good thing when my legs soften beneath me. He holds my weight until I find my footing, hating how much I struggle to breathe from the news. I feel like I've lost my father all over again.

"This is why I didn't say anything. Your mother intended to use your father to break into the witches' coven and rescue Kaira. His existence is temporary, but it seems while under the influence of the power, your father can command zombies."

"So, what?" I abruptly snap. "You thought you'd go without me to rescue my sister and be the hero?" I'm shaking with anger the more I learn. "Would you have even told me about my dad if I didn't bump into him out here?"

"It's not like that at all." His shoulders shoot back, but he's not furious, he just looks remorseful. "I don't want you hurt, especially with you not having your power."

"That wasn't your decision to make," I cry and pull free from him. "This whole time, you knew my father was alive and that my mother was a monster, yet you pretended like nothing happened."

"I'm sorry, Narah, but your mother *was* a monster. She killed so many innocent lives and cursed them not to return to life as the undead, but still took their lives away." He squeezes my arms slightly, almost a declaration of his feelings, except I'm not ready to hear his heartfelt apology.

I pull away from him, resigned he can't change his actions, but that doesn't mean I'm ready to forgive him. Not when my chest aches, grieving all over again for my father. So much time has passed since I lost him, and now he stands there as if all my pain was in vain. I hate my mother for bringing him back, and I hate Ragnar for hiding this from me, but most of all, I hate myself that I still mourn him after all this time. For a long time, I blamed Mom for Dad's death, and now, thanks to her, I get to experience it all over again.

"What do you want to do?" Ragnar asks from behind me, his words flat and broken. "Do you want to join us? Will that make you forgive me?"

"I will join the mission," I state adamantly, twisting my head toward him. "And while we're being honest with each other, you want to know why it's better nothing more happens between us?"

He doesn't respond but stares at me as if he's stopped breathing.

"I'm not too different from my mom. We are both sorceresses, and she told me how to use my power. My power comes from draining people, too. That's where my ability comes from, so as you can see, I'm a monster just like her. With my power, I will hurt people, but without it, I am useless to you."

I don't wait for his response but march across the lawn to the gate to reach Nikos' side, drawing him aside. I'm shaking so hard, I can't walk straight, but I use every inch of strength to hold myself together.

"I'm joining you to rescue my sister, but you need to give me a quick moment so I can tell Jae I'll be out for the day."

He looks at me heavily, wipes a tear sliding down my cheek, and glances up at Ragnar, somewhere behind me, then he gives a tight nod. "We'll wait."

Stone and Crius watch us, but I figure Nikos will fill them in, and I make a hasty retreat into the village. Frantically, I clean away the tears from my eyes, not wanting Jae to see that I've been crying. I just need to tell her I'll be gone for a day, maybe two, but in case something happens to us, I need to ensure the family she's staying with can look after her.

Blinking back fresh tears, I step up to the front door and knock.

You can do this, Narah. Just stop crying.

We're on horseback. Me on Stone's horse with him while Dad is on the back of Crius' horse. Their horse neighs and pauses now and then, well aware something unnatural is on his back. I don't blame the poor creature. Even Crius looks stiff and uncomfortable.

The village is behind us, and we're trotting along the dirt path, me bouncing behind Stone, but I hold on tight in order to not fall over.

I can't stop staring at my dad, who's alongside us. When he meets my gaze, he gives me a weak, awkward smile. We're strangers now, and I can't stop crying when all I want is to have him recognize me, hug me, and tell me how much he missed me. For too long, I cried for him, missing the easy way he laughed, the stories he told us, and the way he loved us.

I'd dreamed of this moment when he'd miraculously come back to us, but not like this... never like this where he stares right through me. It isn't fair to be left alone to carry all the memories, all the hurt, all the emotions for us both while looking into the face of the man who's left me broken and alone in this world.

My life has been a litany of disasters. Maybe I'm one of those people who is meant to always hurt. The old saying that time heals is a lie. It's nothing more than life distracting you from the pain. My crushed heart will never repair.

Ragnar is taking the lead of our charge. My emotions are so jumbled up over him and his men. There's no doubt about the attraction I feel toward them, that they are constantly on my mind. I crave their support and know Ragnar and his men are sorry, but there's been so much tension between us lately.

Is it the right decision to walk away once I have my sister? The thought only multiplies the heaviness in my chest. But can I be with someone who hides secrets from me?

I tuck myself against Stone, my cheek pressed to his back, and blink back the tears, needing to pull myself together. He strokes my hands looped around his middle as we move through the woods quickly, with no one speaking for a long while.

A sharp sound fills my ears, and I perk up to Dad whistling. We're in an open field with the edge of the woods at our rear, far from the village.

"What's going on?" I ask, then notice movement in the woods. A figure emerges from behind a lofty pine, stumbling forward, lurching. I shift my weight on the horse for a better look, and I'm staring at an undead. My stomach curdles.

Ragnar said Dad could command them, but it still fills me with dread, and I tighten my hold on Stone.

"Um, why is he calling the undead now?"

Once more, my thoughts are stolen when an ocean of zombies emerges from the woodland. I shudder and press myself against Stone, instinct screaming for me to run. Stone stiffens against me.

The undead creatures rush toward us in their lopsided, broken runs, some with arms outward as if they're rushing to their feed. Us! There has to be close to two hundred. Shit!

"Maybe we should get moving," I suggest.

Dad whistles at them once more.

"Fucking hell," Crius blurts. "Tell me you're not about to feed us to them?"

"Why would I do that?" Dad answers, straight-faced, genuinely confused by the question. "We need them to save Allie's daughter."

His words stab my heart. He really doesn't remember us.

"I have a shortcut to the witches' compound that will take us there faster," Dad explains. "We need to go now, and they'll run after us."

"Are you sure this will work?" Ragnar is his usual stiff and commanding leader, void of emotions, although when he glances at me, there's a dark pain in his eyes. We haven't exchanged a word since we left the village, and maybe that's for the best. There's too much going on right now to get into another argument.

I swallow hard and look away.

STONE

The tension is through the roof, and to add to the whole shit fight with Narah and Ragnar, we now have an army of undead chasing after us like wolves being delivered to their feed.

This wasn't our initial plan. Narah's dad, Gregory, was supposed to wait for us near the edge of the poisonous woods after he'd showed us the shortcut around the woods to reach the coven, hoping we entered the compound first and found Kaira. It'd been straight-forward.

Then Gregory unleashed the zombies on the witches.

I pray to the moon goddess this new plan works.

Narah clings to me as we race across the open plains. Ragnar, Crius, and Narah's father take the lead to reach the witch's coven, a passage Allie had discovered after tracking the witches' movements. And to think, we spent so much time going through the thick of the poisonous woods the first time when we could have shaved off a full day in our travels if we had known this shortcut.

Entering an adjacent forest, which looks like a dead end with a huge rock face mountain in the distance blocking our path, I'll guess we'll find out soon enough. I'm dubious as fuck, but then again, I'm trapped with the zombies trailing behind us. Even though they've fallen a bit behind, they're still following. I'm not afraid to admit each time I look over my shoulder at the horde, my gut squeezes.

Too late to fucking worry about that shit when we're neck-deep in crap already.

We're going to battle, but not the kind I'm used to. For a change, we're not doing the killing.

I just hope Gregory is right about this, along with not snapping back into full zombie mode on us.

If I had any say in this, I'd call this a close suicide mission because if anything goes wrong, we're fucked. This is why I supported Ragnar that Narah shouldn't be with us right now. Narah is stubborn and tenacious, and after the argument between her and Ragnar near the gate, there was nothing that would stop her from joining us to collect her sister.

She holds onto me tightly, her gorgeous tits rubbing up and down my back with every bump, and I love having her this close. Even with the two breaks we took to rest our horses and let the undead catch up with us, she stayed mostly on her own.

Gregory leads us toward a wall of overgrown bushes, which he tramples with his horse to reveal a tight passage between the rock mountain and forest. Well, I wasn't expecting that. Once we emerge, we travel for another few hours through heavy woodland with a thick canopy overhead. So far, there's no bite of magic over my skin either.

Finally, Crius stops near a thicket of pines, and Narah's father climbs off the horse. His body is twitching, reminding me of his crazed state when he was tearing apart the kitchen. Without more magical blood, how long does he have before turning into one of them, and we're left with an onslaught of the undead.

I tense at our situation, more so because Narah's with us.

With the sun descending, flooding the woods with shadows, our presence is easily concealed, so there's that.

Narah slides off my horse, and I turn to take her hand, helping her.

"You'll feel a bit sore from the long ride."

She half-smiles as she stumbles a bit to catch her footing. Ragnar caught us up on their conversation about where Narah's power really comes from. In truth, all magic comes from somewhere. It doesn't manifest out of pure air.

I draw mine from the elements around me, from nature. Narah will find a way to work with what she's given once she learns to gain back her power, which I doubt she's lost. It's inside her; she just needs to bring it out. Her mother's spell suppressed her power, and it's not as if she's around to ask how to fix it.

I hop down from my horse and stretch my back, my bones cracking. "That feels amazing."

Nikos is at my side. "I'll take your horse. We're releasing them a bit further away. Let's hope they don't go too far."

"Thanks." I pivot toward Narah, who's rubbing her thighs, which would be sore. "Hey, listen," I begin. "I know things are complicated right now, and they suck, but there's no rush to decide on anything. I'll always be by your side."

Her breaths deepen as she turns her head to take in everyone moving toward Ragnar.

"That means a lot. I just have a few things to work through." Her eyes are still red and puffy.

I wish I could put her up in a tree to wait out this mission. Instead, I say, "Stay close by my side. If things go to shit, I'll protect you, but you need to listen to me. Understood?"

She nods without hesitation. Narah's no fool and understands the danger we're all in.

Wrapping my arm around her back, I draw her to my side, the urgency to tuck her away safely hitting me like a torrent, consuming me.

In silence, we join the rest of the group.

"From here, we're on foot. Woods are too dense for horses to pass," Ragnar fills us in. His chin lifts to the passage between two bowed trees, revealing a tight dirt track in the woods that I assume was often traveled by the witches.

Over my shoulder, the first wave of encroaching undead shifts through the woods like shadows. Dread zips up my spine, and I hold Narah tighter against my side.

"Once the undead arrive, there will be no stopping them," Narah's dad says. "Stick close to me, and they won't touch you. Plan is to have them barge into the coven. Then we find Allie's daughter. Once the undead begin feasting, their frenzy will be impossible for me to control, so we must leave."

"That instills me with no confidence," Crius groans.

"I'm not sure I like this plan," Narah mutters, concern on her face, and I agree. "We're putting Kaira in danger. There has to be another way."

"We stick to the original plan," Ragnar states. "A few of us sneak into the compound to find Kaira, and once we give the signal, Gregory will unleash the undead on the witches." He stares up at Gregory. "Can you hold them back for that?"

"I can try," he admits, more uncertain than he sounded at Allie's house.

"Not try," Ragnar demands. "You must."

Silence falls between us until Gregory gives a noncommittal nod.

Fuck, this is going to go bad, isn't it?

"I'll take the lead with Nikos. Crius, you're in the rear with Gregory. Stone and Narah, in the middle. No talking. Let's go."

I nod and look down at Narah, whose face has paled.

"You okay?" I whisper.

"Yep. I'm ready to save my sister." Her voice is shaky, and it's clear she's terrified.

Her bravery impresses me, but I won't let anything touch her. I'll fight every single fucking zombie to protect her. Looking behind us into the darkening woods with so many shadows now moving, that anxiety rapidly climbs through me.

"Um, can we hurry, please?" I'm not ready to get close and personal with zombies.

We fall into formation and speed forward. Each time I look behind us, the shadows of undead are closing in on us. Echoes of their gurgling sounds and their rapid footsteps have me rushing, instinct pressing me to run. I keep Narah in front of me. Sensing movement to my far left, I twist my head to see the first zombie scrambling over the overgrowth, making a shortcut right for us.

"Fuck," Nikos bellows.

"Gregory," I snarl, but the man is already pushing to stand in front of us, whistling, which doesn't stop them. The undead teeter on the spot, snapping their jaws, appearing to fight the instinct to rip into us. More appear behind him, and I don't care what Gregory says. I don't trust that he can keep us safe.

"Change of plan," Gregory announces, his body shuddering once more, his voice crackling. "They're a lot harder to control than I initially thought. Run. We need to get them into the coven before they turn on us."

"Are you fucking with us?" Nikos growls.

"Run," Ragnar snaps, shoving us all to hurry ahead of him.

I grab Narah's hand, and we run. A tremor races down my back, then shudders in my belly and my chest that we let ourselves get into this fucked up position. We must be the dumbest people in the world to have listened to Gregory.

Up ahead, there's no sign of an entry to the coven, and panic strangles me. I search the trees as we sprint past for any low-hanging branches I can throw Narah onto.

Fuck.

14

NIKOS

Nobody listens to me!

My gut instinct was off the charts the moment we found Gregory in Allie's home, then add in the dead bodies, and my alarm bells rang like sirens. I should have made Ragnar listen to me, should have forced the point. Making a deal with zombies is asking for our death.

Case in point—we're running for our lives from the undead and rushing toward another enemy, the witches.

Just fucking great!

I stick to the rear with Ragnar to fend off any of the fuckers if they get too close while Crius and Gregory take charge. Stone protects our most precious cargo—Narah. After her confrontation with Ragnar at the gates, things blew up, and now we're all feeling the aftereffects, the growing tension between them. Where does that leave the rest of us? Up shit's creek, that's where.

Pounding the earth with fast steps, the shadowy cloud of undead draws closer. They're on our heels, their chattering teeth, their groans right on the back of my neck. My skin crawls, and I'm running on pure adrenaline. I sure as fuck won't get eaten alive by these creatures.

"This way," Crius calls out, waving at us to take a sharp turn up ahead.

I lift my head to him, and I'm right there, scrambling forward. The path brings us to an arched passage between two bent trees to an open field. The woods are so closely packed together, they're impenetrable. I throw myself through the arch right behind Narah and Stone.

Crius grabs my arms and hauls to my right. Stone does the same with Ragnar, and we're all tucked in behind Gregory, who whistles at the undead charging into the field toward four-foot walls made of twisted branches that span left and right as far as the eye can see. Beyond the wall lays the coven.

"We need to get in there and save Kaira." Narah's frantic voice sets off my panic. If I wasn't already tense as hell, now I'm about to burst.

"Gregory." Ragnar nudges his shoulder. "*We* need to get in there now before the zombies kill everyone. Move."

The man nods, but I don't miss how much he's twitching, how one of his eyes blinks twice as slow as the other. How much time do we have before he turns on us and loses control of the undead?

We're on the run once more, alongside the lurching zombies. There's nothing like being scared shitless that there are actually undead standing feet from us. Clothes hanging off their emaciated bodies, bones visible through gashes and wounds, missing limbs, empty eye sockets, their groans climb with their hunger.

They'll announce their arrival to the witches, but with how fast they're moving, the attack will still be a complete surprise to them.

The more I look at them, the more I wonder what we're unleashing on this coven.

Are we any better than Allie?

She had kept Gregory alive a lot longer than the witches had Kaira. Considering Gregory knew exactly where we had to go to find the witches and what to do, I'd say Allie had plans to take out the witches on her own. For all I know, she could have had plans to take over the wolf packs as well. I'll never admit this to Narah, but perhaps her mother's death wasn't such a tragedy.

"This way," Gregory barks, steering us to the right while the undead move forward like a raging river, slamming right into the wooden barricade. The few who first hit the walls are attacked with bolts of blue electricity that spark outward, striking their bodies, magic meant to kill anyone who touches the wall.

Falling over, the undead get up just as quickly, but the more they ram against the wall, the more the structure creaks and bows forward. They pile on top of each other, building a mountain for others to climb over.

My gut twists in on itself at how relentless these assholes are.

Slipping farther to the right, just out of sight of the creatures, I survey the surrounding perimeter. All clear.

"We get in there from here," Gregory commands and slaps his hand against the wall.

I expect him to get zapped, but nothing happens.

"The zombies have tripped the spell, and while the witches deal with them, we hurry inside."

Taking Narah's arm, her eyes are huge, and the poor thing's shaking.

"I'll help you over." I squeeze her hand slightly.

"Thank you," she answers softly, looking completely lost.

Stone and Ragnar are already scaling the structure, using the intertwined branches as hand and footholds. Crius shoves Gregory up the wall; the man isn't exactly steady on his feet right now.

"One of the other guys will catch you on the other side," I instruct Narah. "Don't take off until we're all over. Understand?"

"Okay."

Grabbing her waist, I lift her and place her on my shoulders, her legs straddling the back of my neck. What I wouldn't give to be in this exact position but face first in her sweet pussy—life goals. I fight harder to make sure we all survive to achieve them.

"Stand on my shoulders, gorgeous." Stepping up to the wall, I press myself face-first to the structure. "Pull yourself up and over." Next to me, Crius has his hands on Gregory's ass, shoving him up. I might have laughed if I wasn't high on adrenaline and panicked at how vulnerable we are.

Holding onto Narah's legs so she doesn't fall over, she awkwardly gets up, then steps off me and scales the rest of the way to where Ragnar's half dangling over the wall. He hauls her up and over. I exchange glances with Crius, who dusts his shirt, then tosses his plaited dreadlocks out of his face and scowls at me.

"Nice that you got pussy smashed up against the back of your head while I had smelly zombie ass in my face."

I half-chuckle. "Says the guy who got pussy last night while I was stuck talking strategy with that old fart. You won this round, my friend."

"Race you over," he suggests, and I pounce on the chance, scaling the wall like a spider, not shy of whacking Crius in the face with my foot. Growling, he throws himself into me, and we tumble over the top and inside the compound, with him crashing against me.

"Fuck!" I groan, having landed on my back. "Get your fat ass off me."

Crius grins, knowing he won that round and offers me his hand. Taking it, I'm on my feet in seconds and dusting my pants, only to see we're alone.

"Where the fuck are they?" I ask.

"Looks like we're on our own. Let's go witch-hunting."

NARAH

Chaos.

That's the only way to describe the situation.

Undead rush madly through the coven's land, the witches' screams are terrifying, and the heavy stench of magic fills the air, its power biting into my skin. Death against magic. That's what's happening, and we still haven't found Kaira as we dart into the third cottage.

Ragnar and Stone go first to knock anyone out while Dad keeps the zombies away. I'm next to him and keep glancing up at him with a stupid urge to just hug him. It's absurd, especially now, of all places, but my eyes tear up each time he looks at me. I don't need that kind of distraction.

A scream catches my attention from the open lawn in front of the cottage we're in.

Frozen in horror, I watch as a group of zombies plow into two older women who are casting a spell, then swallow them in their feeding frenzy. I knew what would happen, but seeing it leaves me tortured.

I don't know who is good and who is bad. Or are there any good witches in this coven? According to Mom, they all wanted us dead. How can I defend that when I'd seen firsthand how much they wanted my sisters and me dead?

Needing to find Kaira, I whip around to see Stone is cleaning his bloody knuckles on the curtains, and Ragnar is about to punch the life out of a man who's on his knees. There are two other men already on the floor, unconscious.

"Stop," I call out, impatient to find my sister. "Not yet."

"I told you to stay outside," Ragnar roars.

After a gasping exhale, I hurry to the man Ragnar is holding by the throat, and Stone has his hands pinned at his back.

"Kaira," I mutter. "The new witch the High Priestess took in recently. Where is she?"

His blue eyes are huge, knowing if he makes one move, Ragnar will finish him.

"The main hut at the end of homes with a pointy roof." His eyes shift to his left to indicate the direction.

I pull back. "Thank you."

Ragnar smashes his fist into the man's face, sending him sprawling onto his back, but I'm already sprinting out of the house.

Ragnar has Dad, and Stone follows me. Sprinting past the zombies and homes, we see witches fleeing their homes while others are chased down by the undead. We run down the path that runs between the two rows of huts. Dad's whistle carves a path for us amid the sheer number of zombies everywhere.

Ahead, a dark, wooden home with a pointy roof comes into view. I move faster, although it feels as though I'm moving in slow motion.

Kaira, please be there. Please.

There's no delay. Stone goes first, plowing the door open with his shoulder. The wood splits open, and we're inside a large room with a table and cushions on the floor. The scent of burning herbs fills the air, but there's no one there, so Stone charges into the back room.

"Where's the High Priestess?"

"Here," Stone bellows, and we're running, my heart in my throat.

Shoving into the right room, I wrench my gaze over to the large cage.

It's not the High Priestess we find.

It's Kaira.

She's inside the cage, huddled, hugging her knees, not looking at us.

A choked breath escapes my throat as I throw myself onto my knees by the cage.

"Kaira." Tugging at the metal, I find a lock on the large door. "We'll get you out, I promise." I yank at the locked door again, my pulse beating in my ears while I want to scream. The bitch has been keeping my sister caged up like an animal.

She looks up at me, her eyes cloudy but doesn't react. It's as though something has been switched off inside of her, and she's just waiting to be reactivated.

Seeing her this way, a sharp ache slices through my heart.

"Stand back," Stone demands.

I retreat quickly as he slams a rock into the lock. Three strikes later, the padlock breaks away, and I frantically rip the door open and drag my sister out. Stone picks her up, cradling her in his arms. She slumps as though she has no ability to stand on her own.

"Kaira." I cup her face, forcing her to look at me, to remember me.

All I see is emptiness when I look into her eyes.

"What's wrong with her?" Stone asks.

"I think the Priestess has been treating her like a puppet."

"Here, give her this to drink," Ragnar announces, producing a vial filled with something red from his pocket. "According to your mother, it's a curse eraser. She intended to use it when she ambushed the witches with your dad's help."

I blink at the small vial Ragnar hands me. The last time Mom healed us, we died, and I lost my powers.

"Is it safe?" I whisper, while outside, a new onslaught of screams ring in the air.

"What choice do we have?" Ragnar says with urgency. "She takes it now, and the Priestess can't awaken her if she finds us, or she doesn't, and we pray we don't cross paths with the Priestess as we escape."

My stomach hurts, and my head spins. I don't want Kaira harmed, but I also can't have her reawaken to use her powers against us. Seconds feel like hours as I feel the men's eyes on me, their expectations for me to decide. Pulling the cork out of the vial, I lean against my sister.

"Kaira, I need you to drink this for me. Alright?" I place the lip of the vial to her mouth while Ragnar holds her jawline and opens her mouth. What looks like blood slurps into her mouth. It smells rotten, but Kaira swallows it, showing no reaction to the taste, then suddenly, she's convulsing in Stone's arms.

My stomach drops, and I cry out, "Kaira, no, please, no." I grip her arms as her eyes roll back into her head, then she goes completely slack in Stone's arms. "Please, please, Kaira. Don't you dare do this to me."

15

CRIUS

"Fifteen zombies," Nikos states, sticking his chest out like a rooster, standing on the roof of a hut across from the one I'm on.

"Get over yourself. I'm already at twenty-one."

"Fuck off, you are not."

I glance down at the trail of dead zombies in my wake. The animated ones are pawing at the walls of our huts but have no idea how to climb up here on their own. Suckers.

Many of the witches have run. They're not even bothering to cast magic in their fight to save their family because one wrong move and you're eaten. I'd do the same if two hundred undead were unleashed on me.

Nikos and I are on our own without Gregory nearby, and the zombies turn on us, so we change tactics and hunt them as we search for our crew.

"I barely see twelve," he chimes.

"Keep telling yourself that. Anyway, can you see the others from up here?" It's getting on my nerves that we haven't found them yet.

Nikos doesn't respond. He's glancing out in the distance at a dark house with a pointy roof... something the rest of the huts don't have.

"Does that look like Gregory?" He points up ahead to someone who could be him in an argument with who I swear is the High Priestess. My hackles rise, remembering our last encounter when the bitch put a curse on us.

Gregory's sudden cry catches on the wind.

"We need to get to him now." I back up a few steps, then run and hurl myself over to Nikos' roof. Landing, the wooden planks groan under my weight. I nudge Nikos. "If you had your powers, you could call to the elements and give us an upperhand to finish this quickly."

"You think it's not on my mind, too?" Nikos had told us not only Narah's power was gone, but his as well. In fact, the small touch of power I have—nothing even close to what Nikos or Narah have, but something specific which can only be done once—is useless now. I feel nothing within me, no spark of magic. We've been wiped clean by Narah's mother.

"It fucking sucks balls," I growl. "And why we're having to do this old school—fists and steel."

Nikos nods and looks down at all the undead next to his hut.

"See those three huts in front of us," I say. "We're going to jump across them, then run for our lives to Gregory. You ready?"

With a grin, he whips around and sprints to the edge. Propelling himself over in a great leap, he sticks a perfect landing. Asshole.

I chase after him, and we don't pause, needing to put distance between us and the horde. Slamming down on the lawn in front of the last hut, we bolt across the open area toward Gregory. The chattering teeth of the creatures chasing us grow in volume, and there's movement all around us. My gut tightens at the sight.

A spark of magic erupts from the High Priestess, striking Gregory in the chest, and white light curls around his chest like a lasso.

Panic strangles me. Nikos growls, knowing exactly how much shit we're in if Gregory dies.

We come up behind them fast, and I'm close enough now to see the scratches and even bite marks on the priestess's neck and arms. She's been fighting zombies and will become one soon. I don't even want to find out what a powerful High Priestess zombie would be capable of.

Seizing the blade from my belt, I give Nikos a knowing look. He's gripping a knife in his hand as well.

Time to spill blood.

With newfound adrenaline, I throw myself behind the witch, who's wobbling on her feet as Gregory drops to his knees. I can only see the whites of his eyes now.

Hell.

He's almost gone from us, and we have undead on our heels. Their moans escalate, and their pounding foot-steps pummel the earth. Fuck me.

I launch myself at the priestess, exhausted of this shit, Nikos right at my side. Slamming into her back, one hand crashes down on her shoulder to hold her while the other drives my blade into her back, thrusting hard to pierce her black heart.

She shrieks, half-twisting, half-arching in my grip, and the zap of her power strikes my shoulder. I bellow from the burning sting that digs down to my bone as if I'd been struck by lightning. Tossed backward, I hit the ground with a groan.

At that same moment, Nikos jumps on the Priestess' back and in one swift move, slices his blade across her throat. Blood spurts over Gregory's face, and the white lines of magic around the man disappear in a crackling snap.

The High Priestess drops to her knees, then falls to her face, and her body self-combusts. One minute she's there, the next she bursts into a puff of dust that swarms the others who stand on the porch.

"Whoa, what the fuck!" Scrambling to my feet, I hold my shoulder, still stinging from her magic.

Narah and Ragnar dart out of the hunt, followed by Stone carrying someone in his arms. We all witness something that makes no sense.

The dead witch cloud of ash floats directly for them, and they bat it away.

"How the fuck did that just happen?" I mutter, then notice Nikos' by Gregory's side, holding him upright.

All around us, zombies are standing and watching, almost in a frozen state.

"What are they doing?" Ragnar asks, his voice shaken, and I can't blame him.

Not much scares me, but I'd just seen a witch turn into dust before my eyes, and now this...

My attention swings to Narah, who runs to her father, kneeling near him and grabbing his arm. I can't hear what she's saying, but she's crying. My chest tightens at the sight, yet the faint groan of the monsters who've suddenly paused is scaring the hell out of me.

How much longer before they attack us?

Ragnar moves to them while I join Stone, who's carrying Kaira. They found her. Perfect.

"We need to leave like yesterday," I grumble under my breath.

The creatures in front of us only all have eyes for Gregory as if they're somehow stuck.

"The moment he turns, we're all fucked," Stone mumbles.

Not waiting another second, I hurry to Ragnar's side and lean in, whispering, "We gotta go now. Gregory's gonna change any second now."

He cuts me a look filled with dread and nods. "You, Nikos, and Stone head back the way we came. See if you can find our horses. We'll be right behind you."

Narah's crying, grasping onto her dad's arm, but he's shuddering. My heart breaks that she has to say goodbye to her father for a second time. That shit destroys a person. I want to be the person who picks her up and reminds her she is loved... Fuck did I just say the L-word?

"Go," Ragnar growls, and I back away, Nikos joining Stone and me.

We carve our way through the mass of zombies, every hair on my body on end.

"This is fucking freaky as hell, man," I mutter.

"Go faster," Stone says, moving so quickly, Kaira bounces in his arms.

Glancing back quickly, Ragnar is lifting Narah into his arms as she reaches for her father. Her cries pierce the air, and my insides shred at the tragic agony she's going through. Ragnar sprints toward us with her clutched tightly in his arms.

Her dad is lying on the ground, still shuddering.

Time is against us. Nikos and I spring ahead faster, and it isn't long before we burst out of the coven into the woods we'd used to get here.

By some miracle, our horses are in the distance, eating grass in an open patch of land beneath the sun. Surveying the land, I notice a group of figures deeper in the woods, rushing away from our direction. Witches.

Thank fuck. Considering they lost so much today, we are the last thing they care about right now. Maybe later, they'll seek revenge, but not today.

By the time we get the horses reined, I heave for breath. Without a word, Nikos and I get everyone loaded, tying Kaira to Stone's back so she doesn't slide off the horse, then we're off.

My heart's galloping, and I haven't been happier to leave a place. We ride in silence until the woods are a blip behind us. Still, no one stops.

A nagging sensation is prodding my mind, telling me it was too easy. That there is no way, the High Priestess would go down that fast. I keep picturing her self-combusting into dust. Is that a thing witches do when they die? Doesn't seem like it to me.

I want to celebrate her death, yet instinct screams something is very off. The more I think about how she died, the more I'm convinced it's not the last time we'll see her.

16

NARAH

I sit quietly beside Kaira's bed. She's groggy as the pack healer, Flora, tries to get her to drink an herbal concoction. Even though it smells like soil and grass and resembles dirty water, Kaira gulps it down.

Flora is curvy, has red curls, and smiles a lot. The moment she walked into the hut with a huge smile, I felt certain she'd heal my sister. Some people just have peaceful natures, and this woman is the epitome of calm. I already like her.

Sitting on the second bed, only a foot away from Kaira's, Jae's curled up against me, hugging a pillow and watching everything. She burst out crying the moment she saw Kaira and hasn't left her side since. Neither of us has. I've been crying from sheer happiness to have her back. We've all been through so much.

"A couple of days of bed rest, then I'll come back to check on you," Flora says to Kaira, who nods. "You're just exhausted and malnourished, which means eating lots of food to gain your strength back. You need to put some meat on your bones, dear."

"Thank you," I say to the healer while Kaira weakly smiles. I walk her out of the hut, where I whisper to her, "So, she'll be back to normal in no time? You didn't sense anything else strange about her?"

"No, she's just tired." Flora's smile is beautiful and reassuring. "Nothing else out of the ordinary. If anything changes, let me know. She's on the mend. All she needs now is nourishment and lots of love."

"That I can do." Giving my thanks, I shut the door and turn back to my sisters. Jae has crawled into bed with Kaira, and they're chatting softly.

Seeing them together, images of the past flash through my mind, reminding me of a simpler time when ignorance had indeed been bliss. Where just being home with my sisters was all I ever wanted.

So much has changed since then, but for tonight, I let myself focus on my sisters.

I hurry to them and sit on the edge of the bed, staring at my sisters and smiling. I've wiped away the dark marks on her brow from the High Priestess, but there are still small smudges around her eyebrows. When she's better, I'll run her a bath.

"How are you feeling?" I ask, brushing a strand of hair stuck to her clammy forehead.

"Like I just ate grass." She smacks her mouth and licks her teeth. "That stuff was nasty."

Holding on to Kaira's arm for dear life, Jae giggles and stares at her sister as though she can't bear to look away in case she vanishes. My heart melts seeing my sisters so close.

"It smelled pretty bad," I say, my heart beaming at how normal she appears. Gone is the crazy in her eyes, and I don't sense any magic around her. "Want me to bring you some food? Hot tea? Anything?"

"Everything I need is right here." Her hand clasps mine, and she shakes her head. "I just want to be with you two. Just stay with me. When I was under the spell, it felt like I was trapped inside myself, and no matter how much I screamed, no one heard me. So, I thought about you two and all the adventures we'd been through to keep me from losing my mind."

I snort, and Jae laughs. "I'm not sure I'd call living with the Storm Wolves an adventure."

"Well, there was that one time you caught and released the rabbit in our house, and it took us half a day to catch him," Jae reminds me. "Then we found him chewing on your underwear."

"Ah, yes, I forgot about that." Like so many other things recently, I've been too preoccupied with surviving and saving my sisters. A thread of sorrow flares through me at how easily I forgot how to enjoy the small things while I've been on the go for months. With Kaira back, maybe that can finally change.

Kaira just smiles as Jae talks her ear off. She looks pale, with dark shadows under her eyes. My chest tightens each time I picture her trapped in that cage. I wish more than anything I had my power to make the High Priestess suffer for what she's done to my sisters and me.

I should take solace that she's dead, and we never have to deal with her again. I try not to worry about the way she died. I've heard of powerful witches dying in mysterious ways, which has everything to do with how much magic they draw within themselves. Lyra seemed like a power-starved priestess.

She's gone. That's all I care about.

Sidling closer to Kaira, I join their conversation. I never want this moment to end.

Having my sisters back makes it bearable that I lost my father a second time. I've decided not to tell my sisters about him coming back to life. There's nothing from that ordeal that will benefit them but might scar them for life. This world has ruined us enough, and if I can spare them some of the horrors, I'll do it.

Just as Ragnar has attempted to do for me.

RAGNAR

"The witch isn't dead," Crius chimes in, then gulps down several mouthfuls of beer. "We all saw it. People don't explode into dust, no matter who they are."

"There was that one time back home when the witch turned someone into dust," Stone mutters. "So it's not implausible."

Crius' mouth pinches to the side. "We're talking about death, bruh, not a fucking spell. I mean, you, Ragnar, and Nikos got a whiff. What do you think? Did you feel anything magical at the time?"

"I was too busy trying not to choke on it," Nikos croaks. "It was nothing but ash."

"Didn't feel like magic," Stone says. Reaching for the sliced meats and cheese from the platter of food on our table, he builds himself a small tower before stuffing it in his mouth.

I shake my head. "The priestess is gone, but let's keep a close eye on each other and the girls in case something feels wrong."

Crius shrugs. "It feels wrong already. Think about it. Those of us who had magic ability lost it, thanks to Allie. That could be why we're not sensing anything."

"More reason to be careful," I state and help myself to bread smeared in butter and honey. "Anyway, tonight's about celebrating that the wicked witch is dead, and we saved Kaira. Tomorrow, I'll start putting into place actions with the Alpha Mihai to claim nearby territories and packs. We have to move fast before Martell discovers he's lost his connection with the witches."

"And before the witches gather to retaliate," Nikos murmurs.

"Valid point," I answer. "Tonight, let's get drunk and be merry. This is a tremendous win for us."

"Narah should be with us," Stone says, his mouth downturned.

Her absence chokes through me as well.

"Agreed, but her sisters need her tonight. More reason for us to have another celebration." I raise my jug of beer, and the men all do the same. "Skál," we say simultaneously and cheer before gulping down our beers.

"More," Nikos bellows, calling over the barman.

The men break out into a conversation, mostly about Crius declaring he killed the largest number of undead at the coven. His competitiveness is admirable, though I've noticed a change in him over the past few weeks. Starting this mission, his jokes were spiteful and dark, and he constantly spoke to me about when he could finally carry out his magic, an ability he could do only once and would result in him dying. That's how his power worked. He drew extraordinary magic from the earth, but in exchange, he had to pay with his life.

Crius had been in a dark place for a long time after the tragedy with his brother. It wasn't his fucking fault but his parents'. He wouldn't listen to reason and, for a long time, sought his own end. So, I promised him coming on this mission with me would be an end fit for a warrior to enter Valhalla. My intention had been to get him to change his mind and never let him go through with it. For the first time, I'm seeing that hopeful change in him.

Narah is responsible. I've seen changes in all of us since she joined us. She's made us better men. To know she's impacted someone as broken as Crius to where, for weeks, he hasn't asked about finishing himself off is an enormous step.

We've all become entangled, and my heartache of sharing Narah is a burden I'll need to overcome because I can't break Narah's heart, my men's, or my own.

NARAH

Two nights later, Kaira is almost back to her normal self, though she becomes exhausted and short of breath if she does too much, so she's homebound. Jae convinced me that she and Kaira should spend tonight at her friend's home, and when I spoke with the girl's mother, she was more than happy to have them.

That leaves me with a night off, and for once, I don't feel as if my life is hanging in the balance. Well, if I ignore my pining wolf, who has been relentlessly whining for him the last few days.

Sitting near the window in the tavern with Ragnar, red streaks the sky as the sun sets. We're alone, but the others are joining us after running a few errands. Ragnar sinks deeper in his seat, watching me across the long table with an unusual, mischievous expression.

"What's that look for?" I ask, taking a sip of my fruity, red wine.

"You're beautiful." Gone is his dark, broody, serious expression. Now, there's softness in his eyes, blue as the sky after a spring shower.

"Well, you've been too busy to see me the last couple of days, so you might as well enjoy what you've missed." I poke my tongue out at him.

He laughs, throwing his head back, and I completely adore the sounds he makes. My whole body responds–nipples tightening, knees weakening, and my thighs pressing together to heighten the tingle deep in my core.

Of course, my wolf stirs and makes me uncomfortable as she shifts within me, protesting my attraction to Ragnar. Only one wolf exists for her—Martell's. I wished I would have eliminated my ex-fated mate and got him out of my system once and for all.

Leaning on the table, Ragnar places his strong arms crossed on the table in front of him, distracting me. He oozes masculine sexiness, and my pulse quickens every time I look at him.

"A lot has happened since we were alone and really talked, and we didn't exactly leave on the best terms."

"So, now you want to talk about it?" I meet his eyes, determination bubbling through me not to be upset with whichever way the conversation goes. For a change, things have gone well for me, and I need to hold on to those high spirits. I've suffered and grieved enough.

"Yes," he answers, sitting there with the hard line of his jaw and his captivating smile.

"Okay, what do you want to talk about?" I'm already listing things in my mind, but I want him to steer this conversation.

"I never should have held back information about your father and what we discovered about your mother. You were right. It wasn't my place, though I only wanted to protect you, Narah." He reaches across the table and takes my hand, his thumb stroking in small circles. "I'm sorry you had to go through the grief of seeing him in that state. I wanted to keep you safe from that."

My heart eases as his sincere and heartfelt words calm the ache from my loss. My fingers curl around his hand, holding on to him, and my chest tightens as he stares at me. Fuck. It's overwhelming and warming that he apologized. Lately, we've clashed, and I worry things won't work out between us. The thought devastates me.

"That's not on you. It was a decision my mother made. Goddess knows why she did, but I'm not angry with you about it anymore." I bite my lower lip, and my thoughts spill out. "Maybe I overreacted. I mean, I don't want to tell my sisters about my father coming back or what my mother was doing. I want to protect them and understand why you held back that information from me. I kind of lost my mind when I saw my dad."

His hand squeezes mine. "It doesn't ease the pain, but you're not alone."

"Thank you," I murmur softly. "I'm almost embarrassed at how quickly I snapped." My cheeks warm up.

"I just need you to understand that I would never harm you. I would burn down the world to keep you by my side, Narah," he says without hesitation. "You need to learn to trust me."

"I will. Right now, even from across the table, you're too far away."

With the most delicious grin, he stands and moves to sit on the bench next to me. My heart constricts, having him so close, our sides touching. His hand sweeps across my back, holding me near. I love being in his arms, keeping me warm and safe.

"I don't want to argue with you again," he said, rubbing my back. "It fucks up with my head too much." Leaning in, he buries his face in the side of my neck. He licks my ear, then whispers, "And it's been really difficult. I've been dying to fuck you."

My underwear are wet almost instantly. I try to speak, but a moan spills from my lips instead.

He pulls me impossibly close to him, so not even a slice of paper could fit between us. "Now, where were we?"

Every part of my body is heightened, and I fight hard not to climb him like a tree as he strokes my hip. My wolf, who's mad at me, growls in my ear and makes for an interesting experience.

"I need things from you, too," I say when I find my voice. Around him, I have no control of my body. Maybe what I need is a huge distraction like Ragnar to ignore my wolf.

"I know you want me. I'm turning you on right now... I can smell your arousal." He takes my other hand and places it on the growing bulge in his pants. "I need to fuck you."

"Now?" I gasp in shock, yet I'm startled at how easily I keep my hand over his cock and give him a slight squeeze, making him hiss with desire.

He laughs, sounding so confident, while I'm drowning in how much I crave him but also want to confirm where we stand.

"And what about your men?" I slip my hand from his cock, well aware anyone in the room can see us.

"I have no desire to fuck them... only you."

I try to turn to face him, but he holds on to me tightly.

"What about *me* fucking your men?" Holding my breath with anticipation, I wait for his response.

He licks his lips, and there's a hard shiver in his voice when he speaks.

"I have trust issues, Narah." He pauses. "After my fated mate rejected me, I've never felt anything for another woman. She left me for another man, and that shit has fucked with my brain for a long time. So, when I saw you with my men, I tried really hard to accept it, but I fell for you too hard and fast and couldn't cope with having you in their arms and not mine."

I study his hard face, and my breathing accelerates hearing the ache in his voice.

"I'm not your fated mate or theirs, but it doesn't mean I can't be drawn to all four of you." My heart's hammering in my chest, wishing the universe had fated me with Ragnar, not Martell.

"Yeah, I know, but jealousy is a dangerous poison once it hits your bloodstream. After I marked you with my bite, my wolf deemed you ours."

"So, how do I help you?" I swallow the lump in my throat, glancing up at him just as my wolf lifts her head within me, unleashing her pining for Martell. I grind my teeth, needing that asshole dead and out of my wolf's head.

Ragnar says nothing right away, leaving me uncertain. Maybe he's coming to terms that I'll work through this with him.

Looking over my shoulder, he smiles at someone, and I twist around to see Nikos walking inside to join us.

"I have an idea of how you can help me," he whispers in my ear as Nikos approaches us. Suddenly, I have a feeling that his plan is going to take Nikos and me by surprise.

NARAH

"I want Nikos to fuck you," Ragnar states as he closes the door inside our hut.

I blink up at him, convinced I misheard. "Wait, did I hear you right?"

He strolls into the room, his focus on me, where Nikos and I are standing near the couch.

"We talked about trust, Narah, and how hard that's been on me. My men are my family, and if I am going to share you with anyone, it's them. First, I want to watch and see firsthand how I react, to know that I can do this without losing my shit."

He sounds frantic, and I want to know how he'll behave watching Nikos fucking me. Will he go ballistic? I stop myself from asking. I don't think I want to know and prefer to believe it won't get to that stage.

I glance over at Nikos, who's smirking and unbuttoning his shirt. He slides it over his round shoulders, revealing muscles on a tanned chest that has my knees weakening. The tattoos on his powerful arms and even those on the shaved sides of his head have me intrigued, and I make a mental note to ask him what they mean.

The man is enormous, built like a mountain.

He sweeps the dark dreadlocks—twisted across the top of his head like a mohawk—over his shoulder. My stomach flutters crazily as this stunning, half-naked man waits to have sex with me. His gaze trails down my body and fills me with confidence I only gain in the presence of my four men. My pulse quickens, and I draw in a sharp breath at the reality that we're doing this.

Nikos unbuckles his belt, then winks at me, and my underwear is instantly drenched. Nibbling on my lower lip, I stare at this Viking god as he opens his zipper and drops his pants, then kicks them aside. Scars litter his body with an especially long one across his chest, which only adds to his rugged and sexy-as-fuck look. When my gaze falls to his heavy cock, hard and ready, he grabs the base and palms it a few times. A growl rumbles in his chest as his eyes darken with lust.

"Let's do this," he snarls.

"Oh, I see. Talk about romantic," I say sarcastically, still stunned at how thick Nikos is, and we've barely touched. Not that I can talk with how wet I am.

"You want romance?" Nikos mutters, smiling slowly. "I'll strip you with my mouth. How does that sound?"

My knees weaken. He's not a man to waste time, focusing on what he intends to claim—me.

Twisting my head, I find Ragnar sitting comfortably on a chair near the door, legs parted, his arms in his lap, watching intensely.

"Is this what you want?" I ask him.

"Yes. He's going to fuck you until you come," he says with a husky voice that makes me wonder if he's not turned on at the thought. Well, that was promising, accepting me with his men.

My cheeks are burning up. "You're going to just watch?"

"I just ask one thing." The corners of his lips curl upward as he reclines further into his seat, shadows falling over his face. "Your mouth is made to take *my* cock." His eyes glint. "No blowjobs."

"Deal, but I can eat her pussy?" Nikos responds eagerly, moving behind me. Heat pours off his body, as does his shadow.

"Anything you want," he answers with a surprisingly calm voice.

"I think I get a say," I murmur as Nikos' large hands tug on my dress. In one deft move, he rips it off me, leaving me in my underwear. A shiver dances over my skin. Nikos isn't a patient man. His now clawed finger curls under the elastic of my panties at my hip and tears them off so easily, they fall away in shreds. Then he presses his chest against my back, towering over me. My nipples pucker at the sensation of his fingers gliding down my arms.

"I'm going to take such good care of you." My eyes remain on Ragnar, watching from the shadows. There's nothing left to the imagination as I stand naked before him.

Nikos's touch trails to my breasts, cupping and squeezing. He pinches my nipples, tearing a moan from my throat. Stepping around me, he blocks my view of Ragnar.

"You are stunning. You smell so good–like sin—and it's been too long since I spread you with my cock."

Arousal courses through me as his hands cup my face, and he kisses me like an animal. Hard and savage, he bites and licks me, reminding me who is about to fuck me. Nikos may be Ragnar's second in command, but the man is a dominating opponent and likes to stake his claim. The way he's kissing me, he's making sure I never forget him.

I'm going to be bruised tomorrow, yet I want more. I claw at his shoulders as his scent burns me up with desire.

He breaks away from me so fast, I stumble from his absence.

"One moment, my beauty." He strolls across the room to do who knows what.

My gaze lifts to Ragnar, who hasn't moved from his seat, hasn't said a word, but I hear the sharp, ragged intakes of his breath. A shiver of delight licks between my legs. I've never had anyone watch me have sex before.

"Is this what you want?" I ask, squirming under his attention.

"Not yet." Ragnar's voice darkens to a rasp. "I haven't heard you scream."

I smile, knowing I won't be able to help myself when Nikos starts. Nikos is an incredible lover, and I'm panting for him. What will Ragnar do? Join us or go ballistic?

There's a scratch against the wooden floorboards, and I turn my head to find Nikos dragging a whole damn table from the back of the hut to where I'm standing.

"What's going on?"

"Ragnar needs to see all of you." One last push and the heavy table is behind me. "Now, come here, gorgeous."

Hungry hands fall to my hips, and I'm suddenly sitting on the edge of the table, the cold kiss of the wood beneath me. He's kissing me once more, and my pussy tingles, starving for him.

Nikos growls as he leans down, taking mock bites from my neck, followed by a long lick where he's pinched my skin. Making his way to my breasts, he falls to his knees to worship me. Drawing a nipple into his mouth, he works his tongue in light circular motions before flicking it.

I arch my back against his touch, my cheeks flushing wildly at the fire erupting through me, and mewl like a kitten. He makes his way to the other breast while his fingers trace my heated pussy. Desperate, I tilt my hips to give him easier access.

Ragnar's gaze never leaves me, and my skin ripples with goosebumps to have him just sitting there, staring.

Nikos releases my breast from his mouth and guides me to lie back. His hands curl around my ankles, bringing them up and prying them open. I feel the low rumble of his possessive growl in my bones, a sensation that leaves me panting, that such a powerful man reacts to me.

I peer down at my body while he stares at my pussy, holding my thighs apart for Ragnar to see everything.

"You are pure seduction." He slides a finger between the seams of my drenched lips. "I've never seen such a gorgeous pussy." He presses a finger into me.

I can barely breathe, my whole body buzzing. Without hesitation, his mouth is on me, stroking me with light flicks.

I arch, moaning. "That's it, right there. Faster, please."

He watches me with a smile in his eyes, enjoying making me beg—he loves this.

His tongue flickers over my clit, and every nerve between my legs tingles. I hear the quickening of his breath, and when he replaces his fingers with his tongue, I know he's enjoying every second.

My hand falls and slips down to Nikos' mohawk as his face pushes deeper, nose grinding against my clit. I moan with the pleasure shuddering through me as his tongue is deep inside me, finding all the right places to make me shudder helplessly. His finger plays with my ass the whole time, teasing me relentlessly, so when he adds a finger, I scream with pleasure.

The man's a beast. Sucking and grazing me with his teeth, quickening his pace, I lose all control and thrash, completely out of my mind. He made me come so hard, I can't think or move, just gasp for breath and grin. That was fucking amazing.

The smacking sound of his lips and tongue lapping me up is fucking sexy. When Nikos gets to his feet, I glance at Ragnar. His chair has fallen onto its side, and he's pacing behind Nikos, a wild animal, trying to hold back.

I meet Nikos' gaze, and his mouth and nose glisten with my slick. He steps aside as I lay on the table, splayed wide for Ragnar.

"Ragnar," I call to him, but he shakes his head, not even looking at me, and my stomach sinks.

"Fuck her already," Ragnar roars.

I can't make out if we're torturing him to a point where he'll never come back to us or if he's fighting his demons.

"Let me know what you want me to do, Narah." Nikos grips his cock, the tip shining with moisture from his precum. "I'm craving to fuck you, but I need to hear it from you first."

My attention swings from Nikos to Ragnar as they turn toward me.

"I want you both," I answer truthfully, stretching my hand out to my tormented Alpha. It kills me to see jealousy twisting his features.

"She's all of ours," Nikos tells him, his eyes sparkling with the arousal and impatience pulsing within him.

"You want us both?" Ragnar asks with a croaky voice, a thick eyebrow arching. The corners of his mouth look as if they might curl into a grin.

"Yes, now. Get over here," I order him. "Please."

He hesitates, and I tense, ready to get down and go over to him. To my surprise, he squares his shoulders and strolls over, though his face is hard to read.

"Come with me," he says softly. Tucking his hands under my body, he lifts me off the table and gently lowers me to the bed, then strips.

Resting on bent elbows behind me, I watch as he peels his top up and over his head. His body is carved of stone, angles and valleys of muscles everywhere I look. When the boots and pants come off, he's erect and bulging. He wants me, no matter how much he's struggling with his thoughts.

"Come to me," I say.

Nikos remains near the bed, his hand on his cock, watching me with hunger in his eyes. I want to give Ragnar the chance to take the lead until he's comfortable.

Pushing against the bed, he lies over me, presses my legs open with his knee, and positions himself between my spread legs. The tip of cock graces my entrance, and I feel his eagerness.

"I want you... crave you," I purr.

"I'll give you everything you need, Narah." His lips curl into a smirk, then he thrusts into me unceremoniously. I arch against him, my muscles straining, my body quivering. Another thrust, pushing harder and stretching me wider. "Fuck, you're so tight."

Ragnar growls as he plunges his cock deeper. Pain flares, and my body jerks beneath him. His eyes are only on me, he takes me savagely, and it's more enjoyable than I would have expected. He's lost to the frenzy of dominating me and making me his.

Gasping for each breath with each thrust, I turn my head to Nikos and stretch my hand out. "Join us."

Nikos hesitates, and darkness slides over his face as Ragnar rolls us onto our sides, my back to Nikos.

I gasp at the fast movement, my heart hitting the back of my throat.

"Get on the damn bed," Ragnar growls at his second in command, then winks at me, leaving me gushing.

"Does that mean…" I whisper.

He nods. "I'm going to make this work. I can't ignore how much Nikos adores you, and I won't take that from him."

The bedsprings groan as Nikos joins us, moving to lie close behind me. His fingers spear through my hair, turning my head so I'm looking over my shoulder at him.

He steals a kiss as his thick cock settles between my asscheeks.

"About fucking time," Nikos growls.

The three of us shift, finding the right position to make it comfortable for each of us. Ragnar is buried inside me, waiting for Nikos.

"I'm rather enjoying being sandwiched between you two." My body's on fire, and when something thick pushes into my ass, I stiffen.

Nikos works himself into me slowly, but that barely lasts. Ragnar holds me, one hand on my hip, the other nestled under my head. Our legs are a tangled mess, and somehow, our bodies perfectly join.

Caged between two Alphas.

Two cocks deep inside me.

I moan, wanting to be fucked by them.

Our movements find a rhythm after a few trials, then they plunge in and out of me. I shiver as these men claim me as their own. Their hands are all over my body, their mouths on me, licking, kissing.

My legs are weak, and I doubt I'd be able to hold myself up. Nikos sucks my tortured neck while Ragnar kisses me, his tongue sliding into my mouth. They leave me dizzy and flying high as my heart beats faster against my ribcage.

"You guys are bastards," Crius' abrupt voice streams across the room so suddenly, I startle. "From now on, I want to be invited to group sex."

We pause our manic fucking and peer up at Stone and Crius, who are watching us with huge eyes.

"So, sharing is back in the cards?" Stone asks, already toeing off his boots and pawing at his shirt.

"You could say that," Ragnar says with a smile in his voice. Gone is the strain.

He's giving me everything I want.

"Well, you all owe me," Crius blurts, peeling off his clothes.

"Hey, wait," I say, slightly alarmed. "A girl only has so many—"

"Holes," Stone finishes with a smirk. "I'm happy with taking turns, sweetheart."

There's no stopping them, and now I've got four naked guys climbing onto the already squished bed.

"We're going to break the bed," I say, breathing heavily as Crius tosses the pillows aside and crawls to my face, peppering me with kisses.

Stone's at our feet, his hands snaking up my legs.

"There are a lot of cocks in this bed," Ragnar murmurs, sounding slightly annoyed and closing his eyes briefly.

I burst out laughing.

"Isn't it me who's supposed to worry about that?"

Nikos is purring across my neck as his cock slips in and out of my ass, unable to help himself.

We're a bundle of lust, arousal, and excitement.

"Since we're all here,"—Ragnar's jaw twitches—"I want to remove Martell's mark on Narah. My bite alone didn't work, but four of us might do the trick." My breathing grows irregular as Ragnar's eyes fix on me. "What do you say?" He slips out of me, and I immediately miss him.

Falling into their arms had made me easily ignore my wolf's whines, but giving it thought stirs her awake. I hate her pining, and I've had enough of feeling anything but hatred for the asshole.

"Yes," I breathe, bracing myself and trying not to feel suffocated.

Nikos withdraws his cock from me.

"Let's do this then." Rolling onto my back, surrounded by these gorgeous Alphas, I smile. "Take your pick of where you'll bite me." That's all it takes. The men find their perfect positions, and anticipation licks through me.

Nikos nuzzles my neck.

Ragnar licks the softness just above my pelvic bone.

Crius slides down, his tongue leading a path to my breast as he shuffles to my side.

My gorgeous Stone kneels between my legs, looking like the luckiest man in the world, his mouth on my inner thigh.

I swallow hard, my heart beating ridiculously fast.

Trapped by four wolf shifter Alphas, submitting to them.

What have I gotten myself into?

They kiss me, then I feel the sharpness of teeth on my flesh. They bite into me without mercy, and I scream, not expecting it to hurt so much.

Canines sink into flesh, and my wolf growls in response to their assault.

With the deep ache comes arousal I didn't expect, and right on its tail, an electric bite pinches across my skin. I thrash and jolt beneath the guys.

"Stop," I bellow. Something's wrong. Oh Goddess, I have to stop this now.

Sparks of blue light jump from my body and leap out, striking my men.

Silence flatlines between us.

Shouting and panic replace the earlier harmony. The men scramble off the bed in a manic rush, all except Crius.

"I knew your magic would feel fucking amazing. I need more while I'm fucking you."

Truth be told, I love his devotion, but the other three worry me.

Wild, huge eyes, stricken with terror, stare at me incredulously, confused and startled.

Vision blurring, I fight against the fear that I hurt them. So far, none of them have fallen over dead, and they have no injuries, though I don't like the way they're staring at me with fright.

"What just happened?" Ragnar demands.

I take a deep inhale, attempting to come to terms with it myself.

"Bad news is that my wolf still pines for Martell," I say, pulling myself up, attempting to appear as calm as possible while naked and aroused but also startled.

"Good news is, you've brought my magic back."

18

NARAH

At the dinner table in the mess hall, Jae is giggling and whispering to Kaira, who's smiling. She's still healing, and my heart expands with the amount of love I have for them.

I didn't have the courage to tell my sisters about our parents. I chose the cowardly path, saying it had been a mistake, and we never found our mother in the woods. I convinced Jae the information Kaira had received about our mother from the witches had been wrong. I feel horrible, but I'd be bawling my eyes out right now if I told them the truth. I'd do anything to protect my sisters, even carrying the burden of the truth.

My men bring us platters of food from the kitchen. I gawk at them—muscles, ruggedness, and their heavenly, masculine, and sexy scents fill my nostrils. How did I get so lucky? How often does someone get to see their fantasies come to life? For once, everything worked in my favor. I have my sisters, my men, and my magic back.

My attention remains on the men as I nibble on my lower lip, remembering the other night in our hut. I have never been more turned on in my life than having four Alphas trying to fuck me.

"Careful there, Narah," Jae says sarcastically, snatching my attention. "You're drooling down your chin."

I cut her a raised brow, then stick out my tongue. "You should focus on serving the orange juice, sis." That's another thing I haven't spelled out for my sisters—my tangled relationship with the four Alphas. My gut aches, thinking how I'll say out loud that I have four boyfriends.

Don't get me wrong, I'm not embarrassed. Fuck, I want to scream the news from the tallest hut that four men want me, but these are my sisters, and I don't want them to be confused.

"Food's up," Stone announces, setting a wooden platter bursting with cuts of roast and crunchy potatoes drenched in butter in the middle of the table. The aroma has me salivating, and I reach over to steal a small potato wedge before popping it into my mouth. It's hot. Fuck is it hot. I frantically fan my mouth and try to chew it without burning my tongue.

Nikos laughs and sets down a basket overspilling with bread rolls and a bowl of churned butter. More food and drinks are set down around us.

Jae's on her feet, passing the plates around, and I catch Kaira staring at nothing, looking lost. If she was back to her normal self, she'd be stealing the food and being a chatterbox like Jae, but she sits quietly, and her face remains pale. What is she thinking? She watches everything with a child-like curiosity.

Time. She needs more time to heal after the ordeal the High Priestess put her through.

"You going to dig in?" Ragnar asks, nudging me in the ribs as he climbs onto the bench next to me. Crius takes my other side, both mountain men pressing against me, while Stone and Nikos cage in my sisters.

"I still can't believe we're all here like this," I say, smiling. "It's a dream come true."

"That deserves a cheer," Nikos calls out, and everyone grabs their drinks as I take my beer-filled glass.

"Skál," he kicks off, lifting his drink, beer splashing over the rim and down his fingers.

I smile ridiculously and lift mine, along with everyone else. "Skál," I call out in unison before clinking our glasses and taking a long drink

"Can we eat now?" Jae asks, already piling her plate with food. "I'm starving, and with so many wolves at the table, I don't think we have enough food."

I laugh at the comical evil eye she gives each of the guys.

"There's more where that came from," Stone murmurs. "You won't starve, little one."

With everyone else, I lean in and fill my plate. Even Kaira joins in, which is a relief. At first, no one talks as we dive into our meals, all of us starving by the sounds of lips smacking, the tearing of meat, and the clanking of knives on the metal plates.

"So, I'm curious," Jae says in that mischievous voice, and I know she's up to something. "How long will we continue to have four Alphas as our guards? They must have cost you a fortune to hire, sis."

Crius chuckles the loudest as he drops a stripped bone to his plate before stabbing his knife into another piece of meat from the main platter.

"You still have a smart-ass mouth on you, just as I remember," he says. "If you must know, your sister has been struggling to pay us what we're really worth, so we're taking it in other forms."

My mouth drops open. He isn't going to say what I think he's going to say.

"Crius," I hiss.

He waves his hand holding the piece of meat in my face to shut me up.

"Yeah, and what's that?" Jae asks curiously and arrogantly. The girl hasn't changed a bit, and I adore her for it.

"You will clean our clothes and our room for months to come," he finally states, and I burst out laughing.

He had me going there for a moment, but I should have known better. My sisters know every excuse under the sun to get out of doing chores or cleaning.

"Is that so?" Jae huffs. She bites into an ear of barbecued corn, eyeing him with a death glare.

Kaira's eating and smiling at the conversation but not saying a word. A niggling unease uncoils in my chest. Maybe tomorrow, I'll have the healer take another look at her.

"Well, you know what I think," Jae interjects while I moan under my breath at how tender the meat is when it falls apart on my tongue. Next to me, Ragnar gives me a soft smile as he fills my plate with more food. Stone and Nikos are shoving food into their mouths like beasts. I guess everyone's hungry today.

"Go on," Crius eggs her on, then bites into his steak.

"You like my sister," Jae suggests, her cheeks blushing.

I adore how innocent she is while attempting to be tough.

"Narah is *my* mate," Ragnar interrupts, and I stare at him with my heart pounding in my chest at the words I've wanted to hear from my real fated mate for so long. Even my wolf's pining for Martell doesn't throw me off because my heart melts for Ragnar.

"And mine," Crius pipes in.

"Mine, too," Nikos adds.

"Count me in," Stone says.

My sisters' eyes bulge out.

"Well, guess the cat's out of the bag," I say to break the silence. "I was going to tell you both tomorrow, but hey, it's out now."

"You have four boyfriends?" Jae's eyeing me like a hawk. "But you already have a fated mate... Martell." Her brow pinches. "How do you all sleep in the same bed? What about Kaira and me? If you're now officially her new fated mates, will you protect us, too?" She keeps on rattling off questions.

Before I can respond, the men all speak simultaneously with their own variation of how our relationship works, how sharing is commonplace among wolves, how fated mates are not the only chance at love. The more I listen to them, the more I grin wildly at how much thought they've given this.

My sisters aren't freaking out but considering their ideas. I'm surrounded by family talking about my awkward-as-hell love life. This is a lot more entertaining than I would have ever imagined.

As they all chat and laugh, I catch Kaira's gaze.

She's silent, sitting with her hands in her lap and looks at me with an intense look that raises the hairs on my arms.

"Are you okay, sweetie?" I ask.

Her throat moves when she swallows, and she takes a few moments to answer.

"Yeah. I'm fine." Then she returns to eating and joins the conversation.

Something uncomfortable stirs within me... something doesn't feel right.

I lower my gaze and tell myself it's just my paranoid imagination. Tonight is about putting the past behind us.

That's exactly how I want to spend the rest of the night with my new family.

RAGNAR

Coldness from the new day blasts my face and rips at my clothes.

I slow my horse after a frantic race across the field. Over my shoulder, there's no sign of the undead we'd spotted in the distance. They're becoming more commonplace in the Savage Sector, and it's fucking alarming.

My skin crawls as I'm reminded of the tightly enclosed compound in the Shadowlands Sector to keep the zombies out. How long before they swarm everything here, and we have to lock ourselves up behind walls?

"Colt's the leader of the pack we're visiting first, and he's a fucking weasel," Mihai growls under his breath, dragging me from my thoughts. The Alpha of Bane Wolves rides beside me through sparse pine tree woods while his men stay wide to ensure there are no surprise attacks. Nikos takes the lead while Crius remains at our rear.

"Good to know," I reply. "What's Colt's weakness?" We're heading out to visit nearby packs to gain their loyalty.

"Women mostly. He runs the next largest wolf pack after mine, and he's desperate. He has only five females in a pack with close to one hundred males." He casts a glance around us at the sound of twigs snapping. A deer bounces through the woods, away from us. "Unfortu- nately, he's a weasel and untrustworthy."

"So, we offer him some of your forty females but don't deliver until he's completed his mission."

Mihai cuts me a sharp look that could skin me alive. "The forty women you're bringing me are for my pack alone," he growls.

"So, what's the plan then? Promise and don't deliver?" I sneer. I may be as callous as the next Alpha, but in this world, everyone watches, and no one forgets, so I always try to keep my word.

"Not everyone is going to survive *our* takeover of the Savage Sector." Mihai shrugs, a look of disdain washing over his face. "I would think you of all Alphas would know because of where you're from."

I clench my jaw, knowing too well that everyone sees northerners like me as barbaric, but we're no different from the monsters in this country, killing at any chance they can take.

I give a low chuff. "Those in my hometown may be ruthless bastards, but we keep our word."

"Good," Mihai barks. "Then I trust you will keep yours and bring me the forty bitches you promised before the month's up. If you can get more, do so, and I may forgive you for the shit you've pulled with my daughter." There's fury behind his gaze.

I'm fuming on the inside, ready to gouge out his eyes. Mihai pushes me with his uncouth words, and I want to tear his fucking head off. I cast a glance at Mihai's men, who flank us from deeper in the woods, watching us.

One command from me, and my men and I would destroy them. I'd take pleasure in ripping out Mihai's tongue for daring to threaten me. We are far away from the pack and could easily blame their deaths on the undead. No skin off my nose if they die... well, except I need the fuckhead, who has sway over some of the local packs.

Since the damned virus destroyed the world, sectors have burst with male-domineering Alphas who want two things—territory and females—and trust only those in their sectors.

Not strangers like me.

I swallow the rageful words pushing at my throat and lift my attention to Mihai.

"I gave you my word, didn't I?" I snap, my voice darkening. I'm already in a filthy mood. Better we didn't talk, or one of us wouldn't return to the pack.

"You are a manipulative son of a bitch," he gripes. "I get it. Pussy is pussy, and if it wasn't for our damned primal cravings, females would be nothing more than slaves, never to be seen, but we're talking about my daughter."

"Like I said, there's no problem." I tamp down the anger boiling inside me.

"Have you fucked her yet?" he growls abruptly, catching me off guard.

My shoulders rear back, and I snap that time at the ugly bastard. "That's not your business."

"I know you haven't. She told me, crying about you bedding the scrawny wolf girl you brought into my pack. Feed Narah to one of your men. They look sex-starved. Your focus is Lyssa. Remember that."

Hate shifts through me, cold and deadly, and my knuckles turn white, gripping the reins. I crave to shove my fist into his face and rip his spine out for talking about Narah that way.

You need him to take over the Savage Sector.

Fuck! Fuck!

I grind my back teeth.

His beady gaze is on me, expecting to get a rise out of me. Cockhead.

"Narah is not an issue," I hiss through clenched teeth, the words shredding my throat like barbed wire. "What I do before I complete my deal with your daughter is none of your fucking business or hers." I hold the bastard's gaze.

"Do whatever you need." His mouth curls into a menacing grin. "Fuck the girl until you get it out of your system, but you're mating with my daughter. Break our arrangement, and I'll kill you and your men. Better yet, get rid of the girl, or I'll do it for you."

My muscles twitch, and a growl tears through my chest.

"Don't threaten me, Mihai, or this will end only one way." I hold my voice steady, even if my wolf roars within me. "You burned to ashes. We made a deal, so I'll see it through, but you will uphold your end of the fucking bargain—sway over the large packs to our loyalty, and I step into the position of Alpha for Savage Sector. Otherwise, I will destroy your whole pack."

His upper lip thins over sharp canines.

That had been our deal, but the bastard has his eye on a bigger prize. From the beginning, I knew he would be a problem, but I hadn't planned on killing him before I took over reign.

19

NARAH

A distant wolf's cry startles me out of sleep.

"Ragnar?"

I look around the hut but see no sign of my men. They hadn't returned last night from their mission to win over the local pack, and I miss them terribly.

Harsh orange sunlight streams through the window, and I rub my eyes. Pushing my legs out from under the blanket, I'm convinced they'll arrive back today. My throat is as dry as sand, and I'd kill for a hot brew of coffee from the mess hall.

My head is spinning, and something already feels odd about the day. Coffee will help. It should help.

Standing on my bare feet, the floorboards are cold to the touch. Jae's soft snores fill the room as I turn my attention to Kaira's empty cot across the room. Worried, I blink the sleep from my eyes. I quickly cross the room and peel back the messy blanket to find a pillow underneath. No Kaira.

There are no other rooms in this hut, so I can only assume she's gone out to the toilets. Not loving the idea of her going out there alone in a pack crammed with male Alphas and Betas, I quickly change out of my flimsy nightdress. Once in baggy pants and a long-sleeved shirt, I step into my boots.

Stifling a yawn, I shut the door behind me. The morning cold wraps its icy claws around me. Winter is getting closer. How long before the snow starts, and it's freezing? I need to speak with Ragnar about where we'll stay as winter approaches.

Once upon a time, I used to dream of taking Kaira and Jae as far from the Storm Wolves as possible and finding a perfect place to live alone, a safe haven. Maybe I've been too naive or just foolish—no such place exists in our world.

Survival requires strong Alphas. As Ragnar carves out his own territory in Romania, I have to ensure my sisters are out of danger from the war about to break out.

No wolf bends the knee to an Alpha without resistance.

Especially to a foreigner like Ragnar.

So, chaos will ensue between the packs before anything improves. Not to mention how the Storm Wolves will play into this.

That thought awakens my wolf, filling me with a weak whine of longing. The agony she carries for Martell weaves through me. It's a strange sensation to both hate and yearn for someone, against your better judgment.

Wrapping my arms around my middle, I follow the winding, worn path toward the bathhouses. Only a few Alphas are out and about, mostly guards. The smell of porridge cooking in the kitchen floats in the air, and my stomach grumbles.

I pass a dozen homes, about to swing toward the bath huts when the spectacular sky calls to me. Billowy red clouds shine on the horizon as though someone had painted them with blood. It's beautiful in a haunting way. I turn away, but not before something else grabs my attention...a flowing white nightdress.

Blinking, I pause and realize it's Kaira, standing with her back to me in the woods by the river. She crouches by the water, seeming to wash her hands. Her spine pushes against the thin fabric of her dress, her back curved forward, looking so frail, my insides hurt. But with it, ice starts somewhere in the pit of my gut and lingers inside me–a worrying, gnawing sensation that something looks wrong.

Is she sleepwalking and forgot where the bathrooms are? She hasn't walked in her sleep since she was a child.

I shake my head, and the rhythmic beat of my heart picks up its pace. In haste, I cross the open grounds, leaving behind the huts, reminded of the last time I'd been here nights ago with Crius.

Back then, butterflies had burst through my stomach, beating their wings at the emotions he aroused within me.

Now, I'm scared half to death that something is wrong with Kaira. After everything, she deserves peace. *Please let it be nothing.* I swallow hard, my fingers dancing across my middle as I hurry closer.

"Kaira," I call out, needing to know she's alright.

Silence. She doesn't respond. When she finally pulls herself up, I reach for her shoulder.

She's cold to the touch.

My sister slowly turns toward me, a smile in her eyes and licking her lips.

I'm not sure what I'm looking at—the twisted expression on her face, the blood splattered across the front of her white nightdress.

Or the monster I see lingering behind her glare.

Fright slams into me. I've seen this look on her face... but it can't be.

Please, please, let it be a mistake. Please don't let her still be under the High Priestess' spell.

"Kaira..." My voice cracks as my throat thickens, and I fight to still the tremble in my arms. "What have you done?"

Part of me doesn't want a response. I'm not sure if I can take it after everything we've been through after losing our mother and our father twice. I hate the feeling growing within me, hate how it makes my heart race, and hate that it makes me feel vulnerable and think the worst.

Deep inside, I know the truth, and it shreds through me.

Kaira has never been herself, has she?

I fucking knew something had been up with her. I knew it!

I stiffen, and the dance of my wild magic bites down on my arms, and my mind spins. Memories of things Mother taught me about being a sorceress mean nothing when anger and unease hammer my insides.

Kaira's eyes seem to be darker. "Don't worry, sister, this isn't my blood." Her voice is different, like it was before— she's still possessed.

"You're not my sister," I hiss. "How the fuck are you still under the spell? Lyra's dead," I mumble, my hands curling at my sides. The spark of magic dances across my knuckles and feels like barbed wire slicing into my flesh.

I grit my teeth, furious.

"Who said I'm under any spell?" she answers with a wry smirk. "Besides, I think we can call a truce, don't you? And to show you I mean every word, I've done you a favor and removed one of your obstacles." Her piercing stare turns away from me, making it clear she wants me to look in the same direction.

I follow her line of sight to the woods running parallel to the river.

That's when I see Lyssa.

A sob breaks past my throat, bile stirring in my empty stomach.

Lyssa is nailed to a tree trunk. Her lifeless head hanging forward. Her arms are pinned to the tree over her head, and the front of her body is slit open, neck to groin.

Blood stains nearby trees.

I'm suddenly bending over, hurling up bile, every inch of me swallowed by terror. Throwing up an empty stomach hurts, as though someone is gutting me from the inside out, but it doesn't compare to what Kaira... no, what the High Priestess has done.

Fragments of memories slip into my mind—Father back home and the way we'd found him after the Storm Wolves finished beating him. Broken bones and so much blood, he was unrecognizable. If it wasn't for the tattoo on his chest, I could have easily pretended it was someone else.

Terror pulses through me, and I fight the panic rushing over me like undulating waves.

I wipe the mess from my mouth and straighten up, facing Kaira.

She's laughing, her head thrown back.

I'm so livid, I can't see straight.

My hands shoot outward, white lines of magic flashing from my fingertips. The kind I haven't felt for weeks and that makes me feel whole once more. I don't give a fuck where I draw my magic from, as long as I end her now.

Kaira moves with such speed, one second, she's in front of me, then she's at my back, her taloned hand wrapped around my throat, the other digging fingernails into my chest, right over my heart. A bite of magic encases and engulfs me, tightening around me, keeping me locked in place, and making the rest of the world appear hazy, as though we're encased in its cocoon.

I scream with excruciating pain, my magic vanishing in an instant, having nothing to do with me.

"The only reason you're not dead is because of Kaira. The bitch has a strong hold and is fighting me. Thanks to her, you still breathe."

I'm shattered, absolutely devastated. She's possessed my sister this whole time? Bile churns in my gut, knowing I let her spend all that time with Jae.

"What do you want?" My words are barely audible because of her grip on my throat.

"While your sister won't let me destroy you or Jae, I know your enemy wolves are coming for this pack and will rip you to shreds." She cackles in my ear, and I shake with fury. "Besides, I know exactly where to find your mother now...Gregory was very cooperative once I got into his head. She's all I've ever needed–even if dead. She holds the true power I seek. You and your sisters were merely my stepping stone."

I struggle against her magical hold constricting around me, and my breath locks in my lungs.

Her words are like blades, piercing through me, knowing we'd been used this whole time. My sister was abused by the witch just to get to our mother. Untameable fury rises through me, and my wolf shoves forward with a dark anger.

"I'm sorry I can't kill you," she purrs. "But I'll leave you with something just as destructive."

At that moment, I shift, my wolf shaking and emerging.

Something hard strikes me in the back of the head, pain cracking across my skull. My eyes flutter upward, I'm falling, and the world darkens.

"Narah," someone's frantically calling my name and shaking me.

My thoughts bleed into each other, but something stronger comes over me. The smell of sexy, masculine males floods my nostrils and swallows me—so beautiful, so delicious.

Yet the terror of Lyra's return destroys me.

All while a fire blazes over me as if I've been set on fire.

I open my eyes to all four Viking men staring down at me, and my heart races. Ragnar cradles me and sets me on my feet, then tucks me against him so protectively, I gush.

I might enjoy it more if the world would stop spinning as I peer out across the grounds, finding no sign of my sister.

"Why do you smell different?" Stone asks, his nostrils flaring as he sniffs me.

"Fuck, you smell delicious. I could eat you up," Crius purrs in my ear.

Nikos has his hands on me, his eyes morphing into his wolf's with a feral hunger burning behind them.

"I feel strange," I murmur to Ragnar, the earlier fire now racing through my body as if I'm about to self-combust. "I think Lyra did something to me. And she's back. She possessed Kaira this whole time... and the wolves are coming..." I ramble, gasping for air.

"Narah," he growls possessively, not seeming to hear my words. The sound he makes has my knees buckling. His hand slides across my lower back, and a moan slips past my lips. My panties are drenched instantly, and I fall into his arms.

"What the hell is wrong with me?"

His nostrils flare once more when he inhales my scent, and his eyes flutter backward, almost losing himself. His grip tightens while fear pummels me.

"Fuck, we're in huge trouble." His voice deepens. His men are all around me, smelling, touching, and licking me. "This is the worst possible timing, Narah. You'll attract every male in this pack instantly, every male anywhere near you in fact. They'll kill us to get their chance to rut and breed with you. Your scent will drive them insane. Drive us insane."

"Wh-What do you mean?" I gasp, my blood running cold.

"You're going into heat."

GRAB YOUR COPY OF BOOK 4, CURSED WOLF HERE

CURSED WOLF

Start reading book 4, Cursed Wolf.

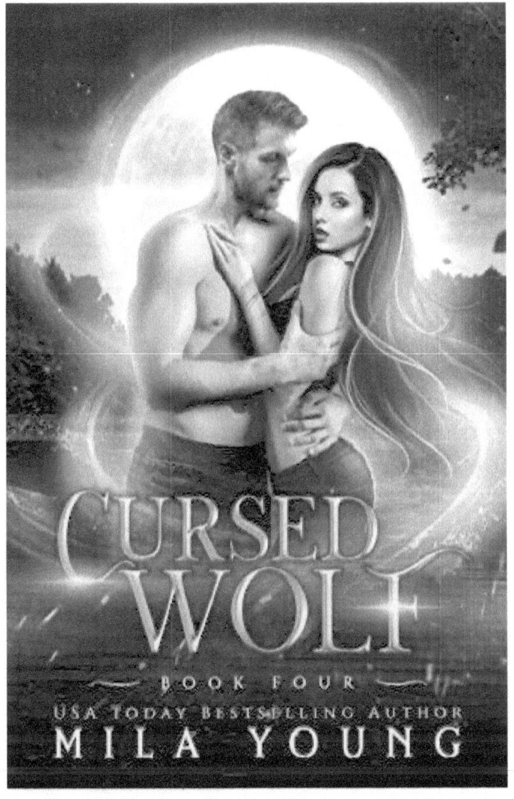

SHADOWLANDS SECTOR

They call me an outcast, weak.

I've fought my whole life for survival, running from an attack on my family I ended up hiding with the Ash Wolves. This one move might be my biggest mistake of all. And I'm the queen of mistakes...

I let them believe I'm broken, let them believe the lies. I let them believe anything they want...as long as it isn't the truth.

There's a monster inside me, one made of teeth and claws and terrifying need. I swallow it down, hiding under the pretense of being normal. But I'm not normal. I'm anything but.

Bonding is the only thing that will save us—me and the Ash

pack. Only I need someone strong enough to fight the darkness inside me...and savage enough to stay.

Will the three ruthless alphas help me...when they find out the truth of what I am?

Shadowlands Sector is book 1 in a shifter paranormal romance story for those who love strong protectors, wolf shifters, and steamy scenes.

Shadowlands Sector and Savage Sector are based in the same shared world.

***

A FREE STORY JUST FOR YOU ....

Did you enjoy Savage Sector and want more? Sign up for my newsletter at www.subscribepage.com/milayoung and you will receive a free novella from me as a thank you gift your joining my newsletter.

In addition, you'll be given special access to deleted and bonus scenes, new release announcements and so much more!

ABOUT MILA YOUNG

**Find all Mila young books at
www.milayoungbooks.com**

Best-selling author, Mila Young tackles everything with the zeal and bravado of the fairytale heroes she grew up reading about. She slays monsters, real and imaginary, like there's no tomorrow. By day she rocks a keyboard as a marketing extraordinaire. At night she battles with her mighty pen-sword, creating fairytale retellings, and sexy ever after tales. In her spare time, she loves pretending she's a mighty warrior, walks on the beach with her dogs, cuddling up with her cats, and devouring every fantasy tale she can get her pinkies on.

Ready to read more and more from Mila Young?
www.subscribepage.com/milayoung

Join Mila's **Wicked Readers group** for exclusive content, latest news, and giveaway.
www.facebook.com/groups/milayoungwickedreaders

For more information...

milayoungauthor@gmail.com